THE GIRL WHO CRIED MONSTER

Look for more Goosebumps books
by R.L. Stine:

Welcome to Dead House
Stay Out of the Basement
Monster Blood
Say Cheese and Die!
The Curse of the Mummy's Tomb
Let's Get Invisible!
Night of the Living Dummy

Goosebumps

THE GIRL WHO CRIED MONSTER

R.L. STINE

AN
APPLE
PAPERBACK

SCHOLASTIC INC.
New York Toronto London Auckland Sydney

ISBN 0-590-46618-6

20   5/9

Printed in the U.S.A.   **40**

First Scholastic printing, May 1993

THE GIRL WHO CRIED MONSTER

I love to scare my little brother, Randy. I tell him scary stories about monsters until he begs me to stop. And I'm always teasing him by pretending to see monsters everywhere.

I guess that's why no one believed me the day I saw a *real* monster.

I guess that's why no one believed me until it was too late, and the monster was right in my own house.

But I'd better not tell the ending of my story at the beginning.

My name is Lucy Dark. I'm twelve. I live with my brother, Randy, who is six, and my parents in a medium-sized house in a medium-sized town called Timberland Falls.

I don't know why it's called Timberland Falls. There are a few forests outside of town, but no one cuts the trees down for timber. And there aren't any falls.

So, why Timberland Falls?

It's a mystery.

We have a redbrick house at the end of our street. There's a tall, overgrown hedge that runs along the side of our house and separates our yard from the Killeens' yard next door. Dad's always talking about how he should trim the hedge, but he never does.

We have a small front yard and a pretty big back yard with a lot of tall, old trees in it. There's an old sassafras tree in the middle of the yard. It's cool and shady under the tree. That's where I like to sit with Randy when there's nothing better to do, and see if I can scare the socks off of him!

It isn't very hard. Randy scares easy.

He looks a lot like me, even though he's a boy. He's got straight black hair just like me, only I wear mine longer. He's short for his age, like me, and just a little bit chubby.

He has a round face, rounder than mine, and big black eyes, which really stand out since we both have such pale white skin.

Mom says Randy has longer eyelashes than mine, which makes me kind of jealous. But my nose is straighter, and my teeth don't stick out as much when I smile. So I guess I shouldn't complain.

Anyway, on a hot afternoon a couple of weeks

ago, Randy and I were sitting under the old sassafras tree, and I was getting ready to scare him to death.

I really didn't have anything better to do. As soon as summer came around this year and school let out, most of my really good friends went away for the summer. I was stuck at home, and so I was pretty lonely.

Randy is usually a total pain. But at least he is somebody to talk to. And someone I can *scare*.

I have a really good imagination. I can dream up the most amazing monsters. And I can make them sound really real.

Mom says with my imagination, maybe I'll be a writer when I grow up.

I really don't know about that.

I *do* know that it doesn't take a whole lot of imagination to frighten Randy.

Usually all I have to do is tell him there's a monster trying on his clothes upstairs in his closet, and Randy turns even whiter than normal and starts shaking all over.

The poor kid. I can even make his teeth chatter. It's unbelievable.

I leaned back against the smooth part of the tree trunk and rested my hands on the grass, and closed my eyes. I was dreaming up a good story to tell my brother.

The grass felt soft and moist against my bare feet. I dug my toes into the dirt.

Randy was wearing denim shorts and a plain white sleeveless T-shirt. He was lying on his side, plucking up blades of grass with one hand.

"Did you ever hear about the Timberland Falls toe-biter?" I asked him, brushing a spider off my white tennis shorts.

"Huh?" He kept pulling up blades of grass one by one, making a little pile.

"There was this monster called the Timberland Falls toe-biter," I told Randy.

"Aw, please, Lucy," he whined. "You said you wouldn't make up any more monster stories."

"No, I'm not!" I told him. "This story isn't made up. It's true."

He looked up at me and made a face. "Yeah. Sure."

"No. Really," I insisted, staring hard into his round, black eyes so he'd know I was sincere. "This is a true story. It really happened. Here. In Timberland Falls."

Randy pulled himself up to a sitting position. "I think I'll go inside and read comic books," he said, tossing down a handful of grass.

Randy has a big comic book collection. But they're all Disney comics and *Archie* comics because the superhero comics are too scary for him.

"The toe-biter showed up one day right next

4

door," I told Randy. I knew once I started the story, he wouldn't leave.

"At the Killeens'?" he asked, his eyes growing wide.

"Yeah. He arrived in the middle of the afternoon. The toe-biter isn't a night monster, you see. He's a day monster. He strikes when the sun is high in the sky. Just like now."

I pointed up through the shimmering tree leaves to the sun, which was high overhead in a clear summer-blue sky.

"A d-day monster?" Randy asked. He turned his head to look at the Killeens' house rising up on the other side of the hedge.

"Don't be scared. It happened a couple of summers ago," I continued. "Becky and Lilah were over there. They were swimming. You know. In that plastic pool their mom inflates for them. The one that half the water always spills out."

"And a monster came?" Randy asked.

"A toe-biter," I told him, keeping my expression very serious and lowering my voice nearly to a whisper. "A toe-biter came crawling across their back yard."

"Where'd he come from?" Randy asked, leaning forward.

I shrugged. "No one knows. You see, the thing about toe-biters is they're very hard to see when they crawl across grass. Because they make themselves the exact color of the grass."

"You mean they're green?" Randy asked, rubbing his pudgy nose.

I shook my head. "They're only green when they creep and crawl over the grass," I replied. "They change their color to match what they're walking on. So you can't see them."

"Well, how big is it?" Randy asked thoughtfully.

"Big," I said. "Bigger than a dog." I watched an ant crawl up my leg, then flicked if off. "No one really knows how big because this monster blends in so well."

"So what happened?" Randy asked, sounding a little breathless. "I mean to Becky and Lilah." Again he glanced over at the Killeens' gray-shingle house.

"Well, they were in their little plastic pool," I continued. "You know. Splashing around. And I guess Becky was lying on her back and had her feet hanging over the side of the pool. And the monster scampered over the grass, nearly invisible. And it saw Becky's toes dangling in the air."

"And — and Becky didn't see the monster?" Randy asked.

I could see he was starting to get real pale and trembly.

"Toe-biters are just so hard to see," I said, keeping my eyes locked on Randy's, keeping my face very straight and solemn.

I took a deep breath and let it out slowly. Just to build up suspense. Then I continued the story.

"Becky didn't notice anything at first. Then she felt a kind of *tickling* feeling. She thought it was the dog licking at her toes. She kicked a little and told the dog to go away.

"But then it didn't tickle so much. It started to hurt. Becky shouted for the dog to stop. But the hurting got even worse. It felt like the dog was chewing on her toes, with very sharp teeth.

"It started to hurt a whole lot. So Becky sat up and pulled her feet into the pool. And . . . when she looked down at her left foot, she saw it."

I stopped and waited for Randy to ask.

"Wh-what?" he asked finally, in a shaky voice. "What did she see?"

I leaned forward and brought my mouth close to his ear. "All the toes were missing from her left foot," I whispered.

"No!" Randy screamed. He jumped to his feet. He was as pale as a ghost, and he looked really scared. "That's not true!"

I shook my head solemnly. I forced myself not to crack a smile. "Ask Becky to take off her left shoe," I told him. "You'll see."

"No! You're lying!" Randy wailed.

"Ask her," I said softly.

And then I glanced down at my feet, and my eyes popped wide with horror. "R-R-Randy —

look!" I stammered and pointed with a trembling hand down to my feet.

Randy uttered a deafening scream when he saw what I was pointing at.

All the toes on my left foot were missing.

2

"Waaaaiiiii!"

Randy let out another terrified wail. Then he took off, running full speed to the house, crying for Mom.

I took off after him. I didn't want to get in trouble for scaring him again.

"Randy — wait! Wait! I'm okay!" I shouted, laughing.

Of course I had my toes buried in the dirt.

He should've been able to figure that out.

But he was too scared to think straight.

"Wait!" I called after him. "I didn't get to show you the monster in the tree!"

He heard that. He stopped and turned around, his face still all twisted up in fright. "Huh?"

"There's a monster up in the tree," I said, pointing to the sassafras tree we'd just been sitting under. "A tree monster. I saw it!"

"No way!" he screamed, and started running again to the house.

"I'll show it to you!" I called, cupping my hands around my mouth so he'd hear me.

He didn't look back. I watched him stumble up the steps to the back stoop and disappear into the house. The screen door slammed hard behind him.

I stood staring at the back of the house, waiting for Randy to poke his frightened head out again. But he didn't.

I burst out laughing. I mean, the toe-biter was one of my best creations. And then digging my toes into the dirt and pretending the monster had gotten me, too — *what a riot!*

Poor Randy. He was just too easy a victim.

And now he was probably in the kitchen, squealing on me to Mom. That meant that real soon I'd be in for another lecture about how it wasn't nice to scare my little brother and fill him full of scary monster stories.

But what else was there to do?

I stood there staring at the house, waiting for one of them to call me in. Suddenly a hand grabbed my shoulder hard from behind. *"Gotcha!"* a voice growled.

"Oh!" I cried out and nearly jumped out of my skin.

A monster!

I spun around — and stared at the laughing face of my friend Aaron Messer.

Aaron giggled his high-pitched giggle till he had tears in his eyes.

I shook my head, frowning. "You didn't scare me," I insisted.

"Oh. Sure," he replied, rolling his blue eyes. "That's why you screamed for help!"

"I *didn't* scream for help," I protested. "I just cried out a little. In surprise. That's all."

Aaron chuckled. "You thought it was a monster. Admit it."

"A monster?" I said, sneering. "Why would I think that?"

"Because that's all you think about," he said smugly. "You're obsessed."

"Oooh. Big word!" I teased him.

He made a face at me. Aaron is my only friend who stuck around this summer. His parents are taking him somewhere out west in a few months. But in the meantime he's stuck like me, just hanging out, trying to fill the time.

Aaron is about a foot taller than me. But who isn't? He has curly red hair and freckles all over his face. He's very skinny, and he wears long, baggy shorts that make him look even skinnier.

"I just saw Randy run into the house. Why was he crying like that?" Aaron asked, glancing to the house.

I could see Randy at the kitchen window, staring out at us.

"I think he saw a monster," I told Aaron.

"Huh? Not monsters again!" Aaron cried. He gave me a playful shove. "Get out of here, Lucy!"

"There's one up in that tree," I said seriously, pointing.

Aaron turned around to look. "You're so dumb," he said, grinning.

"No. Really," I insisted. "There's a real ugly monster. I think it's trapped up there in that tree."

"Lucy, stop it," Aaron said.

"That's what Randy saw," I continued. "That's what made him run screaming into the house."

"You see monsters everywhere," Aaron said. "Don't you ever get tired of it?"

"I'm not kidding this time," I told him. My chin trembled, and my expression turned to outright fear as I gazed over Aaron's shoulder at the broad, leafy sassafras tree. "I'll prove it to you."

"Yeah. Sure," Aaron replied with his usual sarcasm.

"Really. Go get that broom." I motioned to the broom leaning against the back of the house.

"Huh? What for?" Aaron asked.

"Go get the broom," I insisted. "We'll see if we can get the monster down from the tree."

12

"Uh . . . why do we want to do *that*?" Aaron asked. He sounded very hesitant. I could see that he was starting to wonder if I was being serious or not.

"So you'll believe me," I said seriously.

"I don't *believe* in monsters," Aaron replied. "You know that, Lucy. Save your monster stories for Randy. He's just a kid."

"Will you believe me if one drops out of that tree?" I asked.

"Nothing is going to drop out of that tree. Except maybe some leaves," Aaron said.

"Go get the broom and we'll see," I said.

"Okay. Fine." He went trotting toward the house.

I grabbed the broom out of his hand when he brought it over. "Come on," I said, leading the way to the tree. "I hope the monster hasn't climbed away."

Aaron rolled his eyes. "I can't believe I'm going along with this, Lucy. I must be *really* bored!"

"You won't be bored in a second," I promised. "If the tree monster is still up there."

We stepped into the shade of the tree. I moved close to the trunk and gazed up into its leafy green branches. "Whoa. Stay right there." I put my hand on Aaron's chest, holding him back. "It could be dangerous."

"Give me a break," he muttered under his breath.

"I'll try to shake the branch and bring it down," I said.

"Let me get this straight," Aaron said. "You expect me to believe that you're going to take the broom, shake a tree branch, and a monster is going to come tumbling down from up there?"

"Uh-huh." I could see that the broom handle wasn't quite long enough to reach. "I'm going to have to climb up a little," I told Aaron. "Just watch out, okay?"

"Ooh, I'm shaking. I'm *soooo* scared!" Aaron cried, making fun of me.

I shinned up the trunk and pulled myself onto the lowest limb. It took me a while because I had the broom in one hand.

"See any scary monsters up there?" Aaron asked smugly.

"It's up there," I called down, fear creeping into my voice. "It's trapped up there. It's . . . very angry, I think."

Aaron snickered. "You're so dumb."

I pulled myself up to a kneeling position on the limb. Then I raised the broom in front of me.

I lifted it up to the next branch. Higher. Higher.

Then, holding on tightly to the trunk with my free hand, I raised the broom as far as it would go — and pushed it against the tree limb.

14

Success!

I lowered my eyes immediately to watch Aaron.

He let out a deafening shriek of horror as the monster toppled from the tree and landed right on his chest.

3

Well, actually it wasn't a monster that landed with a soft, crackly thud on Aaron's chest.

It was a ratty old bird's nest that some blue jays had built two springs ago.

But Aaron wasn't expecting it. So it gave him a really good scare.

"Gotcha!" I proclaimed after climbing down from the tree.

He scowled at me. His face was a little purple, which made his freckles look really weird. "You and your monsters," he muttered.

That's exactly what my mom said about ten minutes later. Aaron had gone home, and I'd come into the kitchen and pulled a box of juice out of the fridge.

Sure enough, Mom appeared in the doorway, her eyes hard and steely, her expression grim. I could see right away that she was ready to give her "Don't Scare Randy" lecture.

I leaned back against the counter and pretended to listen. The basic idea of the lecture was that my stories were doing permanent harm to my delicate little brother. That I should be encouraging Randy to be brave instead of making him terrified that monsters lurked in every corner.

"But, Mom — I saw a *real* monster under the hedge this morning!" I said.

I don't really know why I said that. I guess I just wanted to interrupt the lecture.

Mom got really exasperated. She threw up her hands and sighed. She has straight, shiny black hair, like Randy and me, and she has green eyes, cat eyes, and a small, feline nose. Whenever Mom starts in on me with one of her lectures, I always picture her as a cat about to pounce.

Don't get me wrong. She's very pretty. And she's a good mom, too.

"I'm going to discuss this with your dad tonight," she said. "Your dad thinks this monster obsession is just a phase you're going through. But I'm not so sure."

"*Life* is just a phase I'm going through," I said softly.

I thought it was pretty clever. But she just glared at me.

Then she reminded me that if I didn't hurry, I'd be late for my Reading Rangers meeting.

I glanced at the clock. She was right. My appointment was for four o'clock.

Reading Rangers is a summer reading program at the town library that Mom and Dad made me enroll in. They said they didn't want me to waste the whole summer. And if I joined this thing at the library, at least I'd read some good books.

The way Reading Rangers works is, I have to go see Mr. Mortman, the librarian, once a week. And I have to give a short report and answer some questions about the book I read that week. I get a gold star for every book I report on.

If I get six gold stars, I get a prize. I think the prize is a book. Big deal, right? But it's just a way to make you read.

I thought I'd read some of the scary mystery novels that all my friends are reading. But no way. Mr. Mortman insists on everyone reading "classics." He means *old* books.

"I'm going to skate over," I told my mom, and hurried to my room to get my Rollerblades.

"You'd better *fly* over!" my mom called up to me. "Hey," she added a few seconds later, "it looks like rain!"

She was always giving me weather reports.

I passed by Randy's room. He was in there in the dark, no lights, the shades pulled. Playing Super Nintendo, as usual.

By the time I got my Rollerblades laced and tied, I had only five minutes to get to the library. Luckily, it was only six or seven blocks away.

I was in big trouble anyway. I had managed to read only four chapters of *Huckleberry Finn*, my book for the week. That meant I was going to have to fake it with Mr. Mortman.

I picked the book up from my shelf. It was a new paperback. I wrinkled up some of the pages near the back to make it look as if I'd read that far. I tucked it into my backpack, along with a pair of sneakers. Then I made my way down the stairs — not easy in Rollerblades — and headed to the Timberland Falls town library.

The library was in a ramshackle old house on the edge of the Timberland woods. The house had belonged to some eccentric old hermit. And when he died, he had no family, so he donated the house to the town. They turned it into a library.

Some kids said the house had been haunted. But kids say that about *every* creepy old house. The library *did* look like a perfect haunted house, though.

It was three stories tall, dark shingled, with a dark, pointy roof between two stone turrets. The house was set back in the trees, as if hiding there. It was always in the shade, always dark and cold inside.

Inside, the old floorboards creaked beneath the thin carpet the town had put down. The high windows let in very little light. And the old wooden bookcases reached nearly to the ceiling. When I edged my way through the narrow aisles between the tall, dark shelves, I always felt as if they were about to close in on me.

I had this frightening feeling that the shelves would lean in on me, cover me up, and I'd be buried there in the darkness forever. Buried under a thousand pounds of dusty, mildewy old books.

But of course that's silly.

It was just a very old house. Very dark and damp. Very creaky. Not as clean as a library should be. Lots of cobwebs and dust.

Mr. Mortman did his best, I guess. But he was kind of creepy, too.

The thing all of us kids hated the most about him was that his hands always seemed to be wet. He would smile at you with those beady little black eyes of his lighting up on his plump, bald head. He would reach out and shake your hand. And his hand was always *sopping*!

When he turned the pages of books, he'd leave wet fingerprints on the corners. His desktop always had small puddles on the top, moist handprints on the leather desk protector.

He was short and round. With that shiny, bald head and those tiny black eyes, he looked a lot like a mole. A wet-pawed mole.

He spoke in a high, scratchy voice. Nearly always whispered. He wasn't a bad guy, really. He seemed to like kids. He wasn't mean or anything. And he *really* liked books.

He was just weird, that's all. He sat on a tall wooden stool that made him hover over his enormous desk. He kept a deep aluminum pan on the side of his desk. Inside the pan were several little turtles, moving around in about an inch of water. "My timid friends," I heard him call them once.

Sometimes he'd pick up one of them and hold it in his pudgy fingers, high in the air, until it tucked itself into its shell. Then he'd gently set it down, a pleased smile on his pale, flabby face.

He sure loved his turtles. I guess they were okay as pets. But they were kind of smelly. I always tried to sit on the other side of the desk, as far away from the turtle pan as I could get.

Well, I skated to the library as fast as I could. I was only a few minutes late when I skated into the cool shade of the library driveway. The sky was clouding over. I sat down on the stone steps and pulled off the Rollerblades. Then I quickly slid into my sneakers and, carrying my Rollerblades, I walked through the front door.

Making my way through the stacks — the tall, narrow shelves at the back of the main reading room — I dropped the skates against the wall. Then I walked quickly through the aisles to Mr. Mortman's desk against the back wall.

He heard my footsteps and immediately glanced up from the pile of books he was stamping with a big rubber stamp. The ceiling light made his bald head shine like a lamp. He smiled. "Hi, Lucy," he said in his squeaky voice. "Be right with you."

I said hi and sat down in the folding chair in front of his desk. I watched him stamp the books. He was wearing a gray turtleneck sweater, which made him look a lot like his pet turtles.

Finally, after glancing at the big, loudly ticking clock on the wall, he turned to me.

"And what did you read for Reading Rangers this week, Lucy?" He leaned over the desk toward me. I could see wet fingerprints on the dark desktop.

"Uh . . . *Huckleberry Finn*." I pulled the book from my backpack and dropped it into my lap.

"Yes, yes. A wonderful book," Mr. Mortman said, glancing at the paperback in my lap. "Don't you agree?"

"Yes," I said quickly. "I really enjoyed it. I . . . couldn't put it down."

That was sort of true. I never picked it up — so how could I put it down?

22

"What did you like best about *Huckleberry Finn?*" Mr. Mortman asked, smiling at me expectantly.

"Uh . . . the description," I told him.

I had my Reading Rangers gold star in my T-shirt pocket. And I had a new book in my backpack — *Frankenstein*, by Mary Shelley.

Maybe I'll read *Frankenstein* out loud to Randy, I thought evilly.

That would probably make his teeth chatter forever!

The late afternoon sun was hidden behind spreading rain clouds. I had walked nearly all the way home when I realized I had forgotten my Rollerblades.

So I turned around and went back. I wasn't sure how late the library stayed open. Mr. Mortman had seemed to be entirely alone in there. I hoped he hadn't decided to close up shop early. I really didn't want to leave my new Rollerblades in there overnight.

I stopped and stared up at the old library. Deep in the shade, it seemed to stare back at me, its dark windows like black, unblinking eyes.

I climbed the stone steps, then hesitated with my hand on the door. I had a sudden chill.

Was it just from stepping into the deep shade?

No. It was something else.

I had a funny feeling. A bad feeling.

I get those sometimes. A signal. A moment of unease.

Like something bad is about to happen.

Shaking it off, I pushed open the creaking old door and stepped into the musty darkness of the library.

4

Shadows danced across the wall as I made my way to the main room. A tree branch tapped noisily against the dust-covered pane of a high window.

The library was silent except for the creaking floorboards beneath my sneakers. As I entered the main room, I could hear the steady *tick-tick-tick* of the wall clock.

The lights had all been turned off.

I thought I felt something scamper across my shoe.

A mouse?

I stopped short and glanced down.

Just a dustball clinging to the base of a bookshelf.

Whoa, Lucy, I scolded myself. It's just a dusty old library. Nothing to get weird about. Don't let your wild imagination take off and lead you into trouble.

Trouble?

I still had that strange feeling. A gentle but insistent gnawing at my stomach. A tug at my chest.

Something isn't right. Something bad is about to happen.

People call them *premonitions*. It's a good vocabulary word for what I was feeling right then.

I found my Rollerblades where I had left them, against the wall back in the stacks. I grabbed them up, eager to get out of that dark, creepy place.

I headed quickly back toward the entrance, tiptoeing for some reason. But a sound made me stop.

I held my breath. And listened.

It was just a cough.

Peering down the narrow aisle, I could see Mr. Mortman hovered over his desk. Well, actually, I could just see part of him — one arm, and some of his face when he leaned to the left.

I was still holding my breath.

The clock *tick-tick-ticked* noisily from across the room. Behind his desk, Mr. Mortman's face moved in and out of blue-purple shadows.

The Rollerblades suddenly felt heavy. I lowered them silently to the floor. Then my curiosity got the better of me, and I took a few steps toward the front.

Mr. Mortman began humming to himself. I didn't recognize the song.

The shadows grew deeper as I approached. Peering down the dark aisle, I saw him holding a large glass jar between his pudgy hands. I was close enough to see that he had a pleasant smile on his face.

Keeping in the shadows, I moved closer.

I like spying on people. It's kind of thrilling, even when they don't do anything very interesting.

Just knowing that you're watching them and they don't know they're being watched is exciting.

Humming to himself, Mr. Mortman held the jar in front of his chest and started to unscrew the top. "Some juicy flies, my timid friends," he announced in his high-pitched voice.

So. The jar was filled with flies.

Suddenly, the room grew much darker as clouds rolled over the late afternoon sun. The light from the window dimmed. Gray shadows rolled over Mr. Mortman and his enormous desk, as if blanketing him in darkness.

From my hidden perch among the shelves, I watched him prepare to feed his turtles.

But wait.

Something was wrong.

My premonition was coming true.

Something *weird* was happening!

As he struggled to unscrew the jar lid, Mr. Mortman's face began to change. His head floated up from his turtleneck and started to expand, like a balloon being inflated.

I uttered a silent gasp as I saw his tiny eyes poke out of his head. The eyes bulged bigger and bigger, until they were as big as doorknobs.

The light from the window grew even dimmer.

The entire room was cast in heavy shadows. The shadows swung and shifted.

I couldn't see well at all. It was like I was watching everything through a dark fog.

Mr. Mortman continued to hum, even as his head bobbed and throbbed above his shoulders and his eyes bulged out as if on stems, poking straight up like insect antennae.

And then his mouth began to twist and grow. It opened wide, like a gaping black hole on the enormous, bobbing head.

Mr. Mortman sang louder now. An eerie, frightening sound, more like animal howling than singing.

He pulled off the lid of the jar and let it fall to the desk. It clanged loudly as it hit the desktop.

I leaned forward, struggling to see. Squinting hard, I saw Mr. Mortman dip his fat hand into the jar. I could hear loud buzzing from the jar. He pulled out a handful of flies.

I could see his eyes bulge even wider.

I could see the gaping black hole that was his mouth.

He held his hand briefly over the turtle cage. I could see the flies, black dots all over his hand. In his palm. On his short, stubby fingers.

I thought he was going to lower his hand to the aluminum pan. I thought he was going to feed the turtles.

But, instead, he jammed the flies into his own mouth.

I shut my eyes and held my hand over my mouth to keep from puking.

Or screaming.

I held my breath, but my heart kept racing.

The shadows lurched and jumped. The darkness seemed to float around me.

I opened my eyes. He was eating another handful of flies, shoving them into his gaping mouth with his fingers, swallowing them whole.

I wanted to shout. I wanted to run.

Mr. Mortman, I realized, was a monster.

5

The shadows seemed to pull away. The sky outside the window brightened, and a gray triangle of light fell over Mr. Mortman's desk.

Opening my eyes, I realized I'd been holding my breath. My chest felt as if it were about to burst. I let the air out slowly and took another deep breath.

Then, without glancing again to the front of the room, I turned and ran. My sneakers thudded over the creaky floors, but I didn't care.

I had to get out of there as fast as I could.

I bolted out the front door of the library onto the stone steps, then down the gravel driveway. I ran as fast as I could, my arms flying wildly at my sides, my black hair blowing behind me.

I didn't stop until I was a block away.

Then I dropped to the curb and waited for my heart to stop pounding like a bass drum.

Heavy rain clouds rolled over the sun again.

The sky became an eerie yellow-black. A station wagon rolled past. Some kids in the back of it called to me, but I didn't raise my head.

I kept seeing the shadowy scene in the library again and again.

Mr. Mortman is a monster.

The words repeated nonstop in my mind.

It can't be, I thought, gazing up at the black clouds so low overhead.

I was seeing things. That had to be it.

All the shadows in the dark library. All the swirling darkness.

It was an optical illusion.

It was my wild imagination.

It was a daydream, a silly fantasy.

No! a loud voice in my head cried.

No, Lucy, you *saw* Mr. Mortman's head bulge. You saw his eyes pop out and grow like hideous toadstools on his ballooning face.

You saw him reach into the fly jar. You heard him humming so happily, so . . . hungrily.

You saw him jam the flies into his mouth. Not one handful, but two.

And maybe he's still in there, eating his fill.

It was dark, Lucy. There were shadows. But you saw what you saw. You saw it all.

Mr. Mortman is a monster.

I climbed to my feet. I felt a cold drop of rain on top of my head.

"Mr. Mortman is a monster." I said it out loud.

I knew I had to tell Mom and Dad as fast as I could. "The librarian is a monster." That's what I'd tell them.

Of course, they'll be shocked. Who *wouldn't* be?

Feeling another raindrop on my head, then one on my shoulder, I started jogging for home. I had gone about half a block when I stopped.

The stupid Rollerblades! I had left them in the library again.

I turned back. A gust of wind blew my hair over my face. I pushed it back with both hands. I was thinking hard, trying to figure out what to do.

Rain pattered softly on the pavement of the street. The cold raindrops felt good on my hot forehead.

I decided to go back to the library and get my skates. This time, I'd make a lot of noise. Make sure Mr. Mortman knew someone was there.

If he heard me coming, I decided, he'd act normal. He wouldn't eat flies in front of me. He wouldn't let his eyes bulge and his head grow like that.

Would he?

I stopped as the library came back into view. I hesitated, staring through the drizzling rain at the old building.

Maybe I should wait and come back tomorrow with my dad.

Wouldn't that be smarter?

No. I decided I wanted my skates. And I was going to get them.

I've always been pretty brave.

The time a bat flew into our house, *I* was the one who yelled and screamed at it and chased it out with a butterfly net.

I'm not afraid of bats. Or snakes. Or bugs.

"Or monsters," I said out loud.

As I walked up to the front of the library, rain pattering softly all around me, I kept telling myself to make a lot of noise. Make sure Mr. Mortman knows you're there, Lucy. Call out to him. Tell him you came back because you left your skates.

He won't let you see that he's a monster if he knows you're there.

He won't hurt you or anything if you give him some warning.

I kept reassuring myself all the way up to the dark, old building. I climbed the stone steps hesitantly.

Then, taking a deep breath, I grabbed the doorknob and started to go in.

6

I turned the knob and pushed, but the door refused to open. I tried again. It took me a while to realize that it was locked.

The library was closed.

The rain pattered softly on the grass as I walked around to the front window. It was high off the ground. I had to pull myself up on the window ledge to look inside.

Darkness. Total darkness.

I felt relieved and disappointed at the same time.

I wanted my skates, but I didn't really want to go back in there. "I'll get them tomorrow," I said out loud.

I lowered myself to the ground. The rain was starting to come down harder, and the wind was picking up, blowing the rain in sheets.

I started to run, my sneakers squishing over the wet grass. I ran all the way home. I was totally drenched by the time I made my way through the front door. My hair was matted down on my head. My T-shirt was soaked through.

"Mom! Dad? Are you home?" I cried.

I ran through the hallway, nearly slipping on the smooth floor, and burst into the kitchen. "A monster!" I cried.

"Huh?" Randy was seated at the kitchen table, snapping a big pile of string beans for Mom. He was the only one who looked up.

Mom and Dad were standing at the counter, rolling little meatballs in their hands. They didn't even turn around.

"A monster!" I screamed again.

"Where?" Randy cried.

"Did you get caught in the rain?" Mom asked.

"Don't you say hi?" Dad asked. "Do you just explode into a room yelling? Don't I get a 'Hi, Dad,' or anything?"

"Hi, Dad," I cried breathlessly. "There's a monster in the library!"

"Lucy, please — " Mom started impatiently.

"What kind of monster?" Randy asked. He had stopped snapping the ends off the beans and was staring hard at me.

Mom finally turned around. "You're soaked!" she cried. "You're dripping all over the floor. Get upstairs and change into dry clothes."

Dad turned, too, a frown on his face. "Your

mother just washed the floor," he muttered.

"*I'm trying to tell you something!*" I shouted, raising my fists in the air.

"No need to scream," Mom scolded. "Get changed. Then tell us."

"But Mr. Mortman is a *monster!*" I cried.

"Can't you save the monster stuff till later? I just got home, and I've got the worst headache," Dad complained. His eyes stared down at the kitchen floor. Small puddles were forming around me on the white linoleum.

"I'm serious!" I insisted. "Mr. Mortman — he's really a monster!"

Randy laughed. "He's funny-looking."

"Randy, it's not nice to make fun of people's looks," Mom said crossly. She turned back to me. "See what you're teaching your little brother? Can't you set a good example?"

"But, Mom!"

"Lucy, please get into dry clothes," Dad pleaded. "Then come down and set the table, okay?"

I was so frustrated! I tilted my head back and let out an angry growl. "Doesn't anyone here *believe* me?" I cried.

"This really isn't the time for your monster stories," Mom said, turning back to her meatballs. "Larry, you're making them too big," she scolded my father. "They're supposed to be small and delicate."

"But I like *big* meatballs," Dad insisted.

No one was paying any attention to me. I turned and stomped angrily out of the kitchen.

"Is Mr. Mortman *really* a monster?" Randy called after me.

"I don't know, and I don't care — about *anything*!" I screamed back. I was just so angry and upset.

They didn't have to ignore me like that.

All they cared about was their stupid meatballs.

Up in my room, I pulled off my wet clothes and tossed them on the floor. I changed into jeans and a tank top.

Is Mr. Mortman really a monster?

Randy's question repeated in my head.

Did I imagine the whole thing? Do I just have monsters on the brain?

It had been so dark and shadowy in the library with all the lights turned off. Maybe Mr. Mortman didn't eat the flies. Maybe he pulled them out of the jar and fed them to his pet turtles.

Maybe I imagined that he ate them.

Maybe his head didn't swell up like a balloon. Maybe his eyes didn't pop out. Maybe that was just a trick of the darkness, the dancing shadows, the dim gray light.

Maybe I need glasses.

Maybe I'm crazy and weird.

"Lucy — hurry down and set the table," my dad called up the stairs.

"Okay. Coming." As I made my way downstairs, I felt all mixed up.

I didn't mention Mr. Mortman at dinner. Actually, Mom brought him up. "What book did you choose to read this week?" she asked.

"*Frankenstein*," I told her.

Dad groaned. "More monsters!" he cried, shaking his head. "Don't you ever get *enough* monsters? You *see* them wherever you go! Do you have to *read* about monsters, too?"

Dad has a big booming voice. Everything about my dad is big. He looks very tough, with a broad chest and powerful-looking arms. When he shouts, the whole house shakes.

"Randy, you did a great job with the string beans," Mom said, quickly changing the subject.

After dinner, I helped Dad with the dishes. Then I went upstairs to my room to start reading *Frankenstein*. I'd seen the old movie of *Frankenstein* on TV, so I knew what it was about. It was about a scientist who builds a monster, and the monster comes to life.

It sounded like my kind of story.

I wondered if it was true.

To my surprise, I found Randy in my room,

sitting on my bed, waiting for me. "What do you want?" I asked. I really don't like him messing around in my room.

"Tell me about Mr. Mortman," he said. I could tell by his face that he was scared and excited at the same time.

I sat down on the edge of the bed. I realized I was eager to tell someone about what had happened in the library. So I told Randy the whole story, starting with how I had to go back there because I'd left my Rollerblades.

Randy was squeezing my pillow against his chest and breathing really hard. The story got him pretty scared, I guess.

I was just finishing the part where Mr. Mortman stuffed a handful of flies into his mouth. Randy gasped. He looked sick.

"Lucy!" My dad burst angrily into the room. "What is your *problem*?"

"Nothing, Dad, I — "

"How many times do we have to tell you not to frighten Randy with your silly monster stories?"

"Silly?" I shrieked. "But, Dad — this one is *true!*"

He made a disgusted face and stood there glaring at me. I expected fire to come shooting out of his nostrils at any minute.

"I — I'm not scared. Really!" Randy protested, coming to my defense. But my poor brother was as white as the pillow he was holding, and trembling all over.

"This is your last warning," Dad said. "I mean it, Lucy. I'm *really* angry." He disappeared back downstairs.

I stared at the doorway where he'd been standing.

I'm really angry, too, I thought.

I'm really angry that no one in this family believes me when I'm being serious.

I knew at that moment that I had no choice.

I had to prove that I wasn't a liar. I had to prove that I wasn't crazy.

I had to *prove* to Mom and Dad that Mr. Mortman was a monster.

7

"What's that?" I asked Aaron.

It was a week later. I had to pass his house to get to the library for my Reading Rangers meeting. I stopped when I saw Aaron in the front yard. He was tossing a blue disc, then catching it when it snapped back at him.

"It's a sort of a Frisbee on a long rubber band," he said. He tossed the disc and it snapped back fast. He missed it and it flew behind him, then snapped back again — and hit him in the back of the head.

"That's not how it's supposed to work exactly," he said, blushing. He started to untangle a knot in the thick rubber band.

"Can I play with you?" I asked.

He shook his head. "No. It's for one person, see."

"It's a one-person Frisbee?" I asked.

"Yeah. Haven't you seen the commercials on

41

TV? You play it by yourself. You throw it and then you catch it."

"But what if someone wants to play *with* you?" I demanded.

"You can't," Aaron answered. "It doesn't work that way."

I thought it was pretty dumb. But Aaron seemed to be having a good time. So I said good-bye and continued on to the library.

It was a beautiful, sunny day. Everything seemed bright and cheerful, golden and summer green.

The library, as usual, was bathed in blue shadows. I'd only been back once since that day. Once *very* quickly, to get my Rollerblades. I stopped at the curb, staring up at it. I felt a sudden chill.

The whole world seemed to grow darker here. Darker and colder.

Just my imagination?

We'll see, I thought. We'll see today what's real and what isn't.

I pulled my backpack off my shoulders and, swinging it by the straps, made my way to the front door. Taking a deep breath, I pushed open the door and stepped inside.

Perched over his desk in the main reading room, Mr. Mortman was just finishing with another Reading Rangers member. It was a girl I knew from school, Ellen Borders.

I watched from the end of a long row of books. Mr. Mortman was saying good-bye. He handed her a gold star. Then he shook Ellen's hand, and I could see her try not to make a disgusted face. His hand was probably sopping wet, as usual.

She said something, and they both laughed. Very jolly.

Ellen said good-bye and headed toward the doorway. I stepped out to greet her. "What book did you get?" I asked after we had said our hellos.

She held it up for me. "It's called *White Fang*," she said.

"It's about a monster?" I guessed.

She laughed. "No, Lucy. It's about a dog."

I thought I saw Mr. Mortman's head lift up when I said the word *monster*.

But I might've imagined that.

I chatted a short while longer with Ellen, who was three books ahead of me this summer. She had only one more to read to get her prize. What a show-off.

I heard the front door close behind her as I took my seat next to Mr. Mortman's desk and pulled *Frankenstein* from my bookbag.

"Did you enjoy it?" Mr. Mortman asked. He had been studying his turtles, but he turned to face me, a friendly smile on his face.

He was wearing another turtleneck, a bright yellow one this time. I noticed that he wore a big, purple ring on one of his pudgy pink fingers. He twirled the ring as he smiled at me.

"It was kind of hard," I said. "But I liked it."

I had read more than half of this one. I would have finished it if it didn't have such tiny type.

"Did you enjoy the description in this book, too?" Mr. Mortman asked, leaning closer to me over the desk.

My eye caught the big jar of flies on the shelf behind him. It was very full.

"Well, yeah," I said. "I kind of expected more action."

"What was your favorite part of the book?" Mr. Mortman asked.

"The monster!" I answered instantly.

I watched his face to see if he reacted to that word. But he didn't even blink. His tiny black eyes remained locked on mine.

"The monster was really great," I said. I decided to test him. "Wouldn't it be neat if there were *real* monsters, Mr. Mortman?"

Again he didn't blink. "Most people wouldn't be too happy about that," he said quietly, twirling his purple ring. "Most people like to get their scares in books or in movies. They don't want their scares to be in real life." He chuckled.

I forced myself to chuckle, too.

I took a deep breath and continued my little test. I was trying to get him to make a slip, to

44

reveal that he wasn't really human. "Do you believe that real monsters exist?" I asked.

Not very subtle. I admit it.

But he didn't seem to notice.

"Do I believe that a scientist such as Dr. Frankenstein could build a living monster?" Mr. Mortman asked. He shook his round, bald head. "We can build robots, but not living creatures."

That wasn't what I meant.

Some other people came into the library. A little girl with her white-haired grandmother. The little girl went skipping to the children's book section. The grandmother picked up a newspaper and carried it to an armchair across the room.

I was very unhappy to see them. I knew that the librarian wouldn't change into a monster while they were here. I was sure he only ate flies when the library was empty. I was going to have to hide somewhere and wait for them to leave.

Mr. Mortman reached into his desk drawer, pulled out a gold star, and handed it to me. I thought he was going to shake my hand, but he didn't. "Have you read *Anne of Green Gables*?" he asked, picking up a book from the pile on his desk.

"No," I said. "Does it have monsters in it?"

He threw back his head and laughed, his chins quivering.

I thought I caught a flash of recognition in his

eyes. A question. A tiny moment of hesitation.

I thought my question brought something strange to his eyes.

But, of course, again it could have been my imagination.

"I don't think you'll find any monsters in this one," he said, still chuckling. He stamped it with his rubber stamp and handed it to me. The cover was moist from where his fingers had been.

I made an appointment for the same time next week. Then I walked out of the main reading room and pretended to leave the library.

I pulled open the front door and let it slam, but I didn't go out. Instead, I crept back, keeping in the shadows. I stopped at the back wall, hidden by a long row of bookshelves.

Where to hide?

I had to find a safe hiding place. Safe from Mr. Mortman's beady eyes. And safe from anyone else who might enter the library.

What was my plan?

Well, I'd been thinking about it all week. But I really didn't have much of a plan. I just wanted to catch him in the act, that's all.

I wanted to see clearly. I wanted to erase all doubts from my mind.

My plan was to hide until the library was empty, to spy on Mr. Mortman, to watch him change into a monster and eat flies again.

Then I'd know I wasn't crazy. Then I'd know my eyes hadn't been playing tricks on me.

On the other side of the room, I could hear the little girl's grandmother calling to Mr. Mortman. "Do you have any spelling books? Samantha only likes picture books. But I want her to learn to spell."

"Grandma, whisper!" Samantha called harshly. "This is a library, remember! Whisper!"

My eyes searched the long, dark shelves for a hiding place. And there it was. A low bookshelf along the floor near the back was empty. It formed a narrow cave that I could crawl into.

Trying to be as silent as I could, I got down on my knees, sat down on the shelf, turned, slid my body back, and tucked myself in.

It wasn't really large enough to stretch out. I had to keep my legs folded. My head was pressed hard against the upright board. Not very comfortable. I knew I couldn't stay like this forever.

But it was late afternoon. Maybe Samantha and her grandmother would leave soon. Maybe I wouldn't have to stay tucked on the shelf like a moldy old book for very long.

My heart was pounding. I could hear Mr. Mortman talking softly to Samantha. I could hear the rustle of the old lady's newspaper. I could hear the *tick-tick-tick* of the big wall clock on the front wall.

I could hear every sound, every creak and groan.

I suddenly had to sneeze. My nose tickled like crazy! There was so much dust down here.

I reached up and squeezed my nose hard between my thumb and forefinger. Somehow I managed to shut off the sneeze.

My heart was pounding even harder. I could hear it over the *tick-tick-tick* of the clock.

Please leave, I thought, wishing Samantha and her grandmother *out* of there.

Please leave. Please leave. Please leave.

I don't know how long I can stay tucked on this dusty shelf.

My neck was already starting to hurt from being pressed against the shelf. And I felt another sneeze coming on.

"This book is too hard. I need an easier one," Samantha was saying to Mr. Mortman.

I heard Mr. Mortman mutter something. I heard shuffling feet. Footsteps.

Were they coming this way?

Were they going to see me?

No. They turned and headed back to the children's section on the side.

"I've already read this one," I heard Samantha complain.

Please leave. Please leave. Please leave.

It must have been only a few minutes later when Samantha and her grandmother left, but it seemed like hours to me.

My neck was stiff. My back ached. My legs were tingling, both asleep.

I heard the front door close behind them.

The library was empty now. Except for Mr. Mortman and me.

I waited. And listened.

I heard the scrape of his tall stool against the floor. Then I heard his footsteps. He coughed.

It suddenly grew darker. He was turning off the lights.

It's show time! I thought.

He's closing up. Now's the time. Now's the time he'll turn into a monster before my eyes.

I rolled silently off the shelf, onto the floor. Then I pulled myself to a standing position. Holding onto a higher shelf, I raised one leg, then the other, trying to get the circulation back.

As the overhead lights went out, most of the library was blanketed in darkness. The only light came from the late afternoon sunlight flooding through the window at the front of the room.

Where was Mr. Mortman?

I heard him cough again. Then he began to hum to himself.

He was closing up.

Holding my breath, I tiptoed closer to his desk. I leaned my side against the shelves as I moved, keeping in the shadows.

Whoa.

I suddenly realized Mr. Mortman wasn't at his desk.

I heard his footsteps behind me, at the back of the main reading room. Then I heard his shoes thud across the floor of the front entryway.

I froze in place, listening hard, still holding my breath.

Was he leaving?

No.

I heard a loud *click*.

The sound of a lock being turned.

He had locked the front door!

I hadn't planned on that. No way. That was definitely *not* part of my plan.

Frozen in the dark aisle, I realized that I was *locked in* with him!

Now what?

8

Maybe my plan wasn't exactly the best plan in the world.

Maybe the whole idea was stupid.

You can bet I had plenty of doubts racing through my mind as I heard Mr. Mortman return to the main reading room.

My plan, of course, was to prove to myself that I was right, that he was a monster. And then — to *run out of the library!*

The plan wasn't to be locked in that dark, creepy building with him, unable to escape.

But here I was.

So far, I was okay. He had no idea that anyone else was here with him. No idea that he was being spied on.

Pressed against the tall shelves, I crept along the narrow aisle until I was as close as I dared to go. I could see his entire desk, caught in a deep orange rectangle of light from the high window.

Mr. Mortman stepped behind his desk, humming softly to himself. He straightened a stack of books, then shoved it to a corner of the desk.

He pulled open his desk drawer and shuffled things around, searching for something in there.

I crept a little closer. I could see very clearly now. The afternoon sunlight made everything orangey-red.

Mr. Mortman tugged at the neck of his turtleneck. He rolled some pencils off the desktop into the open desk drawer. Then he shut the drawer.

This is boring, I thought.

This is very boring. And normal.

I must have been wrong last week. I must have imagined the whole thing.

Mr. Mortman is just a funny little man. He isn't a monster at all.

I sank against the tall shelf, disappointed.

I'd wasted all this time, hiding on that filthy shelf — for nothing.

And now here I was, locked in the library after closing time, watching the librarian clean off his desk.

What a thrill!

I've got to get out of here, I thought. I've been really stupid.

But then I saw Mr. Mortman reach for the fly jar on the shelf behind him.

I swallowed hard. My heart gave a sudden lurch.

A smile crossed Mr. Mortman's pudgy face as he set the big glass jar down in front of him. Then he reached across the desk and, with both hands, pulled the rectangular turtle pan closer.

"Dinnertime, my timid friends," he said in his high, scratchy voice. He grinned down at the turtles. He reached into the pan and splashed the water a bit. "Dinnertime, friends," he repeated.

And, then, as I stared without blinking, stared with my jaw dropping lower and lower in disbelief, his face began to change again.

His round head began to swell up.

His black eyes bulged.

His mouth grew until it became an open black pit.

The enormous head bobbed above the yellow turtleneck. The eyes swam in front of the head. The mouth twisted, opening and closing like an enormous fish mouth.

I was right! I realized.

Mr. Mortman is a monster!

I knew I was right! But no one would believe me.

They'll have to believe me now, I told myself. I'm seeing this so clearly. It's all so bright in the red-orange light.

I'm seeing it. I'm not imagining it.

They'll have to believe me now.

And as I gaped openmouthed at the gross creature the librarian had become, he reached into the fly jar, removed a handful of flies, and shoved them hungrily into his mouth.

"Dinnertime," he rasped, talking as he chewed.

I could hear the buzz of the flies inside the jar.

They were *alive*! The flies were alive, and he was gobbling them up as if they were candy.

I raised my hands and pressed them against the sides of my face as I stared.

"Dinnertime!"

Another handful of flies.

Some of them had escaped. They buzzed loudly around his swollen, bobbing head.

As he chewed and swallowed, Mr. Mortman grabbed at the flies in the air, his tiny hands surprisingly quick. He pulled flies out of the air — one, another, another — and popped them into his enormous gorge of a mouth.

Mr. Mortman's eyes swam out in front of his face.

For a short, terrifying moment, the eyes stopped. They were staring right at me!

I realized I had leaned too far into the aisle.

Had he spotted me?

I jumped back with a gasp of panic.

The bulging black eyes, like undulating toadstools, remained in place for another second or two. Then they continued rolling and swimming about.

After a third handful of flies, Mr. Mortman closed the jar, licking his black lips with a snake-like, pencil-thin tongue.

The buzzing stopped.

The room was silent again except for the ticking clock and my thundering heartbeats.

Now what? I thought.

Is that it?

No.

"Dinnertime, my timid friends," the librarian said in a thin, trembling voice, the voice seeming to bob along with the enormous head.

He reached a hand into the pan and picked up one of the little green-shelled turtles. I could see the turtle's legs racing.

Is he going to feed some flies to the turtles now? I wondered.

Mr. Mortman held the turtle higher, studying it with his bulging, rolling eyes. He held it up to the sunlight. The turtle's legs continued to move.

Then he popped the turtle into his mouth.

I heard the crack of the shell as Mr. Mortman bit down.

He chewed noisily, several times, making a loud *crunch* with each chew. Then I saw him swallow once, twice, till he got it down.

I'd seen enough.

More than enough.

I turned away. I began to make my way blindly back through the dark aisle. I jogged quickly. I didn't really care if he heard me or not.

I just had to get out of there.

Out into the sunlight and fresh air.

Away from the crunching sound that kept repeating in my ears. The crunch of the turtle shell as Mr. Mortman chewed it and chewed it.

Chewed it alive.

I ran from the main reading room, my heart thudding, my legs feeling heavy as stone.

I was gasping for breath when I reached the front entry. I ran to the door and grabbed the handle.

And then remembered.

The door was locked.

I couldn't get out.

I was locked in.

And, then, as I stood staring straight ahead at the closed door, my hand gripping the brass knob, I heard footsteps. Behind me. Rapid footsteps.

Mr. Mortman had heard me.

I was trapped.

9

I froze in panic, staring at the door until it became a dark blur in front of me.

Mr. Mortman's footsteps grew louder behind me.

Help! I uttered a silent plea. *Somebody — help me!*

The librarian would burst into the front entryway any second. And there I'd be. Trapped at the door.

Trapped like a rat. Or like a turtle!

And then what?

Would he grab me up like one of his pets?

Would he crunch me between his teeth?

There had to be a way out of there. There *had* to be!

And, then, staring at the blur of the door, it suddenly came clear to me. It all came back in focus. And I realized that maybe — just maybe — I wasn't trapped at all.

Mr. Mortman had locked the door from the inside.

The *inside*.

That meant that maybe I could unlock it and open the door.

If the door locked with a key, then I was stuck.

But if it was just an ordinary lock that you turned . . .

"Hey, is someone out there?" Mr. Mortman's raspy voice burst into my thoughts.

My eyes frantically searched the door. I found the lock under the brass knob.

I reached for it.

Please turn. Please turn. Please turn.

The lock turned in my hand with a soft click. The prettiest sound I ever heard!

In a second, I had pulled open the door. In another second, I was out on the stone steps. Then, I was running as fast as I could, running across the front lawn, cutting through some shrubs, diving through a hedge — running for my life!

Gasping for air, I turned halfway down the block. I could see Mr. Mortman, a shadowy figure in the library door. He was standing in the doorway, staring out, not moving. Just standing there.

Had he seen me?

Did he know it was me spying on him?

I didn't want to know. I just wanted to get away.

The late afternoon sun was ducking behind the trees, making the shadows long and dark. I lowered my head and ran into the long, blue shadows, my sneakers thudding hard against the sidewalk.

I was out. I was okay. I had seen the monster, but he hadn't seen me. I hoped.

I ran until I got to Aaron's house. He was still in the front yard. He was sitting on the stump of an old tree his parents had removed. I could see the blue Frisbee-type thing in his lap. He was struggling to untangle the long rubber band.

Aaron had his head down, concentrating on undoing the knots, and didn't see me at first.

"Aaron — Mr. Mortman is a monster!" I cried breathlessly.

"Huh?" He looked up, startled.

"Mr. Mortman — he's a monster!" I repeated, panting like a dog. I put my hands on my knees and leaned forward, trying to catch my breath.

"Lucy, what's your problem?" Aaron muttered, returning his attention to the rubber band.

"Listen to me!" I screamed impatiently. I didn't sound like myself. I didn't recognize my shrill, panicky voice.

"This thing stinks," Aaron muttered. "It's totally tangled."

"Aaron, *please!*" I pleaded. "I was in the library. I saw him. He changed into a monster. He ate one of his turtles!"

Aaron laughed. "Yum!" he said. "Did you bring *me* one?"

"Aaron, it isn't funny!" I cried, still out of breath. "I — I was so scared. He's a monster. He really is. I thought I was locked in with him. I thought — "

"Tell you what," Aaron said, still picking at the knots in the rubber band. He held the blue plastic disc up to me. "If you can untangle this big knot, I'll let you play with it."

"Aaaaaagh!" I let out an angry scream. *"Why don't you listen to me?"*

"Lucy, give me a break," Aaron said, still holding the disc up to me. "I don't want to talk about monsters now. It's kind of babyish, you know?"

"But, Aaron!"

"Why don't you save that stuff for Randy?" Aaron suggested. He waved the blue disc. "Do you want to help me with this or not?"

"Not!" I screamed. Then I added: "You're a *lousy* friend!"

He looked a little surprised.

I didn't wait for him to say anything else. I took off again, heading for home.

I was really angry. What was *his* problem, anyway? You're supposed to take a friend seriously. You're not supposed to think automatically that your friend is just making up a story.

Couldn't Aaron see how frightened and upset I was? Couldn't he see that it wasn't a joke?

He's a total jerk, I decided, as my house finally came into view. I'm never speaking to him again.

I ran up the driveway, pulled open the screen door, and burst into the house. "Mom! Dad!" My heart was pounding so hard, my mouth was so dry, my cry was a hoarse whisper.

"Mom — where are you?"

I ran through the house until I found Randy in the den. He was lying on the floor, his face two inches in front of the TV, watching a Bugs Bunny cartoon.

"Where are Mom and Dad?" I cried breathlessly.

He ignored me. Just stared at his cartoon. The colors from the TV danced over his face.

"Randy — where *are* they?" I repeated frantically.

"Grocery shopping," he muttered without turning around.

"But I have to talk to them!" I said. "When did they leave? When will they be back?"

He shrugged without removing his eyes from the screen. "I don't know."

"But, Randy!"

"Leave me alone," he whined. "I'm watching a cartoon."

"But I saw a monster!" I screamed. "A real one!"

His eyes went wide. His mouth dropped open. "A real monster?" he stammered.

"Yes!" I cried.

"Did he follow you home?" Randy asked, turning pale.

"I hope not!" I exclaimed. I wheeled around and ran out of the den. I glanced out the living room window as I hurried past. No sign of my parents' car.

So I ran up to my room.

I was so upset. So angry and upset.

I took two steps into my room, then stopped.

There in my bed, under the covers, lay a big, hairy monster, its gnarled brown head on my pillow, its gaping, toothless mouth twisted in an evil grin.

I grabbed the top of my dresser and uttered a loud gasp of shock.

The monster stared at me, one round eye bigger than the other. It didn't move off my pillow.

It uttered a high-pitched giggle.

I mean, I *thought* it giggled. It took me a short while to realize that the giggling was coming from behind me.

I spun around to see Randy just outside the door. When he saw the terrified look on my face, his giggle became a roar of laughter.

"Like it?" he asked, stepping past me into the room and walking up to my bed. "I made it in art class."

"Huh?"

Randy picked up the lumpy brown monster head. As soon as he picked it up, I saw that the hair was brown yarn, that the face was painted on.

"It's papier-mâché," Randy announced proudly. "Neat, huh?"

I let out a long sigh and slumped onto the edge of the bed. "Yeah. Neat," I muttered unhappily.

"I put the pillows under your covers to make it look like he had a body," Randy continued, grinning. His grin looked a lot like the grin on the monster head.

"Very clever," I said bitterly. "Listen, Randy, I just had a really scary thing happen. And I'm really not in the mood for jokes."

His grin grew wider. He tossed the brown monster head at me.

I caught it and held it in my lap. He motioned for me to toss it back, but I didn't.

"Didn't you hear me?" I cried. "I'm very upset. I saw a monster. A real one. In the library."

"You're just embarrassed because my monster head fooled you," Randy said. "You're mad because I really scared you."

"Mr. Mortman is a monster," I told him, bouncing the monster head in my lap. "I saw him change into a monster. His head grew big, and his eyes popped out, and his mouth twisted open."

"Stop it!" Randy cried, starting to look scared.

"I saw him eat flies," I continued. "Handfuls of flies."

"Flies?" Randy asked. "Yuck!"

"And then I saw him pick up one of his pet

turtles. You know. The ones he keeps in that pan on his desk. I saw him pop it in his mouth and eat it."

Randy shuddered. He stared at me thoughtfully. For a moment, I thought maybe he believed me. But then his expression changed, and he shook his head.

"No way, Lucy. You're just mad because I scared you for once. So now you're trying to scare me. But it isn't going to work."

Randy grabbed the monster head from my lap and started out the door. "I don't believe you about Mr. Mortman."

"But it's true!" I protested shrilly.

"I'm missing my cartoons," he said.

Just then, I heard a knock at the front door.

"Mom!" I cried. I leapt off the bed and went tearing to the stairs. I shoved Randy out of my way, and practically flew down the steps, taking them three at a time.

"Mom! Dad — you're home! I have to tell you — "

I froze in front of the screen door.

It wasn't my parents.

It was Mr. Mortman.

11

My first thought was to *run*.

My next thought was to slam the front door.

My next thought was to run back upstairs and hide in my room.

But it was too late to hide. Mr. Mortman had already seen me. He was staring at me through the screen door with those beady black eyes, an evil, thin-lipped smile on his pale, round face.

He saw me, I realized.

He saw me spying on him in the library.

He saw me running away.

He knows that I know his secret. He knows that I know he's a monster.

And he's come to get me.

He's come to get rid of me, to make sure his secret is safe.

"Lucy?" he called.

I stared at him through the screen.

I could see in his eyes that he knew it had been me in the library.

The sun had nearly gone down. The sky behind him was sunset-purple. His face looked even paler than usual in the evening light.

"Lucy, hi. It's me," he said.

He was waiting for me to say something. But I was frozen there in panic, trying to decide whether to run or scream. Or both.

Randy had stopped halfway down the stairs. "Who is it?" he asked.

"It's Mr. Mortman," I replied softly.

"Oh." That was what my little brother said. He came the rest of the way down, then walked past me on his way back to the den.

"Hi, Mr. Mortman," I managed to say, not moving any closer to the door. Then I blurted out, "My parents aren't home."

I knew instantly that it was a dumb thing to say.

Now the monster knew that Randy and I were here alone.

Why did I say that? I asked myself. *How could I be so stupid?*

"I didn't come to see your parents," Mr. Mortman said softly. "I came to see you, Lucy."

He knows! I thought. *He really knows!*

I'm dead meat!

I swallowed hard. I didn't know what to say. My eyes searched the front hallway for a weapon, something to hit him with when he broke through the screen door and came after me.

Mr. Mortman's eyes narrowed. His smile faded.

This is it! I thought.

There was nothing around that I could use to fight him off. A little glass flower vase. That's all I could see. I didn't think it would be too effective against a roaring monster.

"Lucy, I believe this belongs to you," Mr. Mortman said. He held up my blue canvas backpack.

"Huh?"

"I found it back in the stacks," Mr. Mortman said, his smile returning. "I didn't know who had left it. But I found your name and address on the tag here."

"You — you mean — ?" I stammered.

"I always walk home after I close the library, so I thought I'd bring it to you," he said.

Was this a trap?

I studied his face warily. I couldn't tell *what* he was thinking.

I had no choice. I pushed open the screen door, and he handed me the backpack. "Wow. Thanks," I said. "That was really nice of you."

He straightened the sleeves of his yellow turtleneck. "Well, I figured you'd probably want to get started on *Anne of Green Gables* tonight," he said.

"Yeah. Sure," I replied uncertainly.

"I guess you ran out of the library pretty quickly," Mr. Mortman said, staring into my eyes.

"Uh . . . yeah. I had to get home," I told him, glancing back to the den. The cartoon music floated into the hallway.

"So you didn't wait around or anything after our appointment?" he asked.

Does he know? I wonder.

Or is he just trying to find out if it was me or not?

"No," I said, trying to keep my voice from shaking. "I ran right out. I was in a hurry. I — I guess that's why I forgot my bag."

"Oh, I see," Mr. Mortman replied thoughtfully, rubbing his chins.

"Why?" I blurted out.

The question seemed to surprise him. "Oh, it's nothing, really," he said. "I think someone was playing a trick on me. Staying in the library after closing."

"Really?" I asked, opening my eyes wide and trying to sound as innocent as possible. "Why would they do that?"

"To scare me," Mr. Mortman answered, chuckling. "Some kids don't have anything better to do than try to scare the kindly old librarian."

But you're *not* a kindly old librarian, I thought. You're a *monster*!

"I got up to look around," Mr. Mortman continued, "and whoever it was high-tailed it." He chuckled again.

"I wouldn't want to be locked in there overnight," I said, studying his face, hoping my innocent act was working.

"Neither would I!" he exclaimed. "It's a pretty creepy old building! Sometimes I get so scared from all the strange creaks and groans."

Yeah. Sure! I thought sarcastically.

Behind him, I saw my parents' car turn into the driveway. I breathed a silent sigh of relief. Thank *goodness* they were finally home!

"Guess I'll say good night," Mr. Mortman said pleasantly. He turned and watched as my parents rolled past him up the driveway, heading to the back of the house.

"Thanks for bringing the bag," I said, eager to go greet Mom and Dad.

"No problem. See you next week." He hurried away.

I went running to the kitchen. Mom was just coming in through the kitchen door, carrying a brown grocery bag. "Wasn't that Mr. Mortman at the front door?" she asked, surprised.

"Yeah," I answered eagerly. "I'm so glad to see you, Mom. I have to tell you — "

"What did he want?" Mom interrupted.

"He . . . uh . . . returned my backpac — I left it at the library, see. I have to tell you about him, Mom. He — "

"That was really nice of him," Mom said, setting the grocery bag down on the counter. "How come you forgot it, Lucy?"

"I ran out of there really fast, Mom. You see — "

"Well, that was really nice of Mr. Mortman," she interrupted again. She started to remove things from the grocery bag. "He doesn't live in this direction. I think he lives way over on the north side."

"Mom, I'm *trying* to tell you something!" I cried impatiently. My hands were balled into tight fists. My heart was pounding. "Mr. Mortman is a monster!"

"Huh?" She turned away from the counter and stared at me.

"He's a monster, Mom! A real one!" I cried.

"Lucy, Lucy." She shook her head. "You see monsters everywhere."

"Mom!"

"Stop it, Lucy. Stop being dumb. I hope you were polite to Mr. Mortman."

"Mo-om!"

"Enough. Go outside and help your father bring in the rest of the groceries."

12

So, once again my wonderful parents refused to believe me.

I tried to describe what I had seen from my hiding place in the library. But Mom just shook her head. Dad said I had a great imagination. Even Randy refused to be scared. He told Mom and Dad how he had scared me with his stupid papier-mâché monster head.

I practically begged them to believe me.

But Mom said I was just lazy. She said I was making up the story about Mr. Mortman so I could get out of the Reading Rangers program and wouldn't have to read any more books this summer.

When she said that, I got really insulted, of course. I yelled something back. And it ended up with all of us growling and snapping at each other, followed by me storming up to my room.

Slumped unhappily on my bed, I thought hard about my predicament.

I could see that they were never going to believe me.

I had told too many monster stories, played too many monster jokes.

So, I realized, I needed someone else to tell my parents about Mr. Mortman. I needed someone else to see Mr. Mortman become a monster. I needed someone else to *believe* the truth with me.

Aaron.

If Aaron came along with me and hid in the library and saw Mr. Mortman eat flies and turtles with his bulging head — then Aaron could tell my parents.

And they'd believe Aaron.

They had no reason *not* to believe Aaron. He was a serious, no-nonsense guy. My most serious, no-nonsense friend.

Aaron was definitely the answer to my problem.

Aaron would finally make my parents realize the truth about Mr. Mortman.

I called him immediately.

I told him I needed him to come hide in the library and spy on Mr. Mortman.

"When?" he asked. "At your next Reading Rangers meeting?"

"No. I can't wait a whole week," I said, whispering into the phone, even though my parents

74

were downstairs and there was no one around. "How about tomorrow afternoon? Just before closing time. Around five."

"It's too dumb," Aaron insisted. "I don't think I want to."

"I'll *pay* you!" I blurted out.

"How much?" he asked.

What a friend!

"Five dollars," I said reluctantly. I never save much of my allowance. I wondered if I still had five dollars in my drawer.

"Well, okay," Aaron agreed. "Five dollars. In advance."

"And you'll hide with me and then tell my parents everything you see?" I asked.

"Yeah. Okay. But I still think it's dumb." He was silent for a moment. "And what if we get caught?" he asked after a while.

"We'll be careful," I said, feeling a little chill of fear.

13

I spent most of the next day hanging around, teasing Randy. I couldn't wait for the afternoon to roll around.

I was so excited. And nervous.

I had it all worked out. Aaron and I would sneak into the main reading room without Mr. Mortman knowing anyone had come in. We'd hide in the dark shelves, just as I had done.

Then, when the librarian turned off the lights and closed up the library, we'd sneak up the aisle, keeping in the shadows, and watch him become a monster.

Then we wouldn't run out the way I had done. That was far too risky. We would go back to our hiding places in the low shelves and wait for Mr. Mortman to leave. Once he was gone, Aaron and I would let ourselves out of the library and hurry to my house to tell my parents what we had seen.

Easy. Nothing to it, I kept telling myself.

But I was so nervous, so eager to get it over with, I arrived at Aaron's house an hour early. I rang the bell.

No answer.

I rang it again.

Finally, after a long wait, Aaron's teenage brother, Burt, pulled open the door. He had on blue denim shorts and no shirt. "Hi," he said, scratching his chest. "You looking for Aaron?"

"Yeah." I nodded.

"He isn't home."

"Huh?" I practically fell off the porch. "Where is he? I mean, when will he be back?"

"Don't know. He went to the dentist," Burt said, gazing past me to the street.

"He did?"

"Yeah. He had an appointment. With the orthodontist. He's getting braces. Didn't he tell you?"

"No," I said glumly. I could feel my heart sink to my knees. "I was supposed to meet him."

"Guess he forgot," Burt said with a shrug. "You know Aaron. He never remembers stuff like that."

"Well. Thanks," I muttered unhappily. I said good-bye and trudged back down to the sidewalk.

That dirty traitor.

I felt really betrayed.

I had waited all day. I was so *psyched* for spying on Mr. Mortman.

I had counted on Aaron. And all the while, he

had a stupid orthodontist appointment.

"I hope your braces really hurt!" I shouted out loud.

I kicked a small rock across the sidewalk. I felt like kicking a *lot* of rocks. I felt like kicking Aaron.

I turned and headed home, thinking all kinds of ugly thoughts. I was at the bottom of my driveway when an idea popped into my head.

I didn't need Aaron, I suddenly realized.

I had a camera.

My parents had given me a really good camera last Christmas.

If I sneaked into the library with the camera and took a few snapshots of Mr. Mortman after he became a monster, the photos would be all the proof I needed.

My parents would *have* to believe actual color snapshots.

Forgetting my disappointment about Aaron, I hurried up to my room and pulled the camera off the shelf. It already had film in it. I had taken a bunch of shots at Randy's birthday party just before school let out.

I examined it carefully. There were still eight or nine shots left on the roll.

That should be plenty to capture Mr. Mortman at his ugliest.

I glanced at the clock on my desk. It was still

early. A little after four-thirty. I had half an hour before the library closed.

"This has *got* to work," I said out loud, crossing my fingers on both hands.

Then I strapped the camera around my neck and headed to the library.

I entered the library silently and crept to the doorway of the main reading room. My plan was to sneak into the low shelf where I had hidden before. But I quickly saw that it wasn't going to be as easy as I thought.

The library was very crowded. There were several kids in the children's book section. There were people thumbing through the magazines. One of the microfiche machines was being used against one wall. And several aisles, including the one with my special hiding place, had people in them, browsing and searching the shelves.

I'll just have to wait them out, I decided, turning and pretending to search one of the back shelves.

I could see Mr. Mortman standing behind his desk. He was checking out a stack of books for a young woman, opening the covers, stamping the card, then slamming the covers shut.

It was nearly five o'clock. Just about closing time.

I crept along the back wall, searching for another hiding spot. Near the corner, I spotted a large wooden cabinet. I recognized it as I stepped behind it and lowered myself from view. It was the long, tall cabinet that held the card catalogue.

It will hide me quite nicely, I thought.

I hunched down behind the old cabinet and waited. Time dragged by. Every second seemed like an hour.

At five-fifteen, Mr. Mortman was still checking out books for people. He announced closing time, but some of the magazine readers seemed very reluctant to leave.

I felt myself getting more and more nervous. My hands were ice cold. The camera suddenly seemed to weigh a thousand pounds, like a dead weight around my neck. I removed it and dropped it to my lap.

It will all be worth it, I kept repeating to myself.

It will all be worth it if I get a good, clear shot of the monster.

I leaned against the back of the cabinet and waited, my hand gripping the camera in my lap.

Finally, the room emptied out.

I climbed to my knees, suddenly very alert, as I heard the librarian go to lock the front door. A few seconds later, I heard him return to his desk.

I stood up and peered around the side of the

cabinet. He was busily shuffling papers, straightening his desk for the night.

In a few minutes, I hoped, it would be feeding time.

Monster time.

Taking a deep breath, I gripped the camera tightly in one hand and, feeling my heart start to pound, began to make my way silently toward Mr. Mortman's desk at the front of the room.

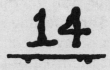

14

Everything seemed to be taking so long today.

Was time really in slow motion? Or did everything seem so slow because my pulse was racing so fast?

I was so eager to get my proof — and get out of there!

But Mr. Mortman was taking his good old time. He shuffled through a stack of papers, reading some of them, folding some of them in half, and tossing them in the wire trash basket beside his desk.

He hummed to himself as he read through the entire stack. Finally, he got to the bottom of the pile and tossed the final sheet away.

Now! I thought. *Now you'll start your monster routine, won't you, Mr. Mortman!*

But no.

He lifted a stack of books from his desk and carried them to the shelves. Humming loudly, he began returning the books to their places.

I pressed myself into the shadows, hoping he wouldn't come to my row. I was near the far wall in front of the row of microfiche machines.

Please, let's get on with it! I begged silently.

But when he finished with the first stack, Mr. Mortman returned to his desk and hoisted up another pile of books to replace.

I'm going to be late for dinner, I realized with a growing sense of dread. My parents are going to *kill* me!

The thought made me chuckle. Here I was, locked inside this creepy old library with a monster, and I was worried about getting scolded for being late for dinner!

I could hear Mr. Mortman, but I couldn't see him. He was somewhere among the rows of shelves, replacing books.

Suddenly his humming grew louder.

I realized he was in the next aisle. I could see him over the tops of the books on the shelf to my right.

And that meant *he* could see *me*!

Gripped with panic, I ducked and dropped to the floor.

Had he heard me? Had he seen me?

I didn't move. I didn't breathe.

He continued to hum to himself. The sound grew fainter as he moved in the other direction.

Letting out a silent sigh of relief, I climbed back to my feet. Gripping the camera tightly in my right hand, I peered around the side of the shelf.

I heard his shoes shuffling along the floor. He reappeared, his bald head shiny in the late afternoon sunlight from the window, and made his way slowly to his desk.

The clock on the wall ticked noisily.

My hand gripping the camera was cold and clammy.

Watching him shuffle things around inside his desk drawer, I suddenly lost my nerve.

This is stupid, I thought. A really bad idea.

I'm going to be caught.

As soon as I step out to snap the picture, he'll see me.

He'll chase after me. He won't let me get out of the library with this camera.

He won't let me get out of here *alive*.

Turn and run! a voice inside my head commanded.

Quick, while you have the chance — turn and run!

Then another voice interrupted that one. *He isn't going to turn into a monster tonight, Lucy,* the voice said. *You're wasting your time. You're getting yourself all nervous and scared for no reason.*

My mind was spinning, whirring with voices

and frightening thoughts. I leaned hard against the wooden shelf, steadying myself. I closed my eyes for a moment, trying to clear my head.

How many shots can you take? a voice in my head asked. *Can you shoot off three or four before he realizes what is happening?*

You only need one good shot, another voice told me. *One good clear shot will be the proof you need.*

You'd better hope he's humming very loudly, another voice said. *Otherwise, he'll hear your camera shutter click.*

Turn and run! another voice repeated. *Turn and run!*

You only need one good shot.

Don't let him hear your shutter click.

I stepped forward and peered around the shelf.

Mr. Mortman, humming happily away, was reaching for the fly jar.

Yes! I cried silently. *Finally!*

"Dinnertime, my timid friends," I heard him say in a pleasant singsong. And as he started to unscrew the jar lid, his head began to grow.

His eyes bulged. His mouth twisted open and enlarged.

In a few seconds, his monstrous head was bobbing above his shirt. His snakelike tongue flicked out of his black mouth as he removed the jar lid and pulled out a handful of flies.

"Dinnertime, my timid friends!"

Picture time! I thought, gathering my courage.

I raised the camera to my eye with a trembling hand. I gripped it tightly with both hands to keep it from shaking.

Then, holding my breath, I leaned as far forward as I could.

Mr. Mortman was downing his first handful of flies, chewing noisily, humming as he chewed.

I struggled to center him in the viewfinder.

I was so nervous, the camera was shaking all over the place!

I'm so glad he's humming, I thought, raising my finger to the shutter button.

He won't hear the camera click.

I'll be able to take more than one shot.

Okay. Okay . . .

He was still enjoying his first batch of tender flies.

Now! I told myself.

I was about to push the button — when Mr. Mortman suddenly turned away.

With a gasp, I stopped myself just in time.

My pulse was pounding at my temples so hard, I could barely see straight.

What was he doing?

He was reaching for another jar. He set it down on his desk and unscrewed the lid.

I raised the camera again and squinted at him through the viewfinder.

What did he have in this jar? Something was fluttering in there. It took me a while to realize they were moths. White moths.

He closed his fist around one and shoved it hungrily into his mouth. Another moth fluttered out of the jar before he could close the lid.

Mr. Mortman's eyes bulged like toadstools growing out of his balloonlike head. His mouth twisted and coiled as he chewed the moth.

Taking another deep breath and holding it, I leaned forward as far as I could, steadied the camera in front of my eye — and snapped the shutter.

15

The FLASH!

I had forgotten about the flash!

I was so worried about the click of the shutter, I had totally forgotten that my camera had automatic flash!

The instant flash of white light made Mr. Mortman cry out angrily. Startled, he raised his hands to cover his bulging eyes.

I stood frozen in the aisle, frozen by carelessness, frozen by my stupidity!

"*Who's* there?" he growled, still covering his eyes.

I realized he hadn't seen me yet. Those big eyes must have been very sensitive to light. The flash had momentarily blinded him.

He let out a monstrous roar that echoed off the four walls of the vast room.

Somehow I revived my senses enough to pull myself back, out of view.

"Who's there?" he repeated, his voice a rasping snarl. "You won't get away!"

I saw him lumbering in my direction. As he lurched toward me, his body swayed awkwardly, as if his eyes were still blinded.

I gaped in horror as he approached.

He seemed steadier with each step. His bulging eyes searched the rows of shelves. He was breathing hard, each breath a furious growl.

"Who's there? Who's there?"

Get going! I told myself, still gripping the camera in both hands. *Get going! What are you waiting for?*

"You won't get away!" the monster cried.

Oh, yes, I will!

He was three rows away, his eyes peering down the dark aisles. Searching. Searching.

He hadn't seen me, I knew. The light of the flash had startled him, then blinded him.

He didn't know it was me.

Now all I had to do was run. All I had to do was get out of there with the proof safely in my hands.

So what was I waiting for?

He lumbered closer. He was only a row away.

Run! I ordered my paralyzed legs. *Run! Don't just stand there!*

I spun around, clumsily bumped into a shelf of books. Several books toppled to the floor.

Run! Don't stop!

It was taking me so long to move. I was so weighed down by my fear.

Run! Lucy! He's right behind you!

Finally, my legs started to cooperate.

Holding the camera in one hand, I began to run through the dark aisle toward the back of the room.

"You won't get away!" the monster bellowed from the next aisle. "I hear you! I know where you are!"

Uttering an animal cry of terror, I ran blindly to the end of the aisle, turned toward the doorway — and crashed into a low book cart.

The cart toppled over as I fell on top of it.

I landed hard on my stomach and knees. The camera bounced from my hand and slid across the floor.

"I've got you now!" the monster growled, moving quickly from the next aisle.

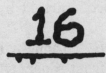

16

I scrambled to get up, but my leg was caught in the cart.

The monster lumbered toward me, panting loudly.

Once again, my fear tried to paralyze me. I tried to push myself up with both hands, but my body felt as if it weighed a thousand pounds.

I'm dead meat! I thought.

Finally, I pushed myself up and freed myself from the cart.

Dead meat. Dead meat.

The panting, growling monster was only a few yards away now, lurching out of a row of shelves.

I grabbed the camera and stumbled to the door, my knee throbbing, my head whirring.

I'll never make it. Never.

And then I heard the loud electronic ringing.

At first, I thought it was an alarm.

But then I realized it was the telephone.

I pulled myself into the doorway and turned.

The monster hesitated at the end of the aisle. His bulbous, black eyes floated up above his face. His gaping mouth, drooling green liquid, twisted into an O of surprise.

He stopped short, startled by the sudden interruption.

Saved by the bell! I thought happily. I pulled open the heavy front door and burst out to freedom.

I ran for two blocks, my sneakers slapping the pavement, my heart refusing to slow its frantic beat. I closed my eyes as I ran, enjoying the feel of the warm, fresh air on my face, the warmth of the late afternoon sun, the sweep of my hair flying behind me as I ran. Feeling *free*. Free and safe!

When I opened my eyes and slowed my pace, I realized that I was gripping the camera so tightly, my hands hurt.

My proof. I had my proof.

One snapshot. One snapshot that nearly cost me my life. But I had it in the camera, my proof that Mr. Mortman was a monster.

"I have to get it developed," I said out loud. "Fast."

I jogged the rest of the way home, cradling the camera under my arm.

As my house came into view, I had a chilling

feeling that Mr. Mortman would be waiting there. That he would be waiting beside the front porch, waiting to grab the camera from me, to rob me of my proof.

I hesitated at the bottom of the driveway.

No one there.

Was he hiding in the bushes? Around the side of the house?

I walked up the front lawn slowly. *You're being stupid,* I scolded myself. *How could Mr. Mortman get here before you?*

Besides, I wasn't even sure he had recognized me.

The lights were out in the library. The room was dark. The closest he had come was the aisle next to mine. And he was blinded for a long while from the camera flash.

I started to breathe a little easier. Yes, it was possible that the librarian didn't know who he was chasing. It was possible that he never got a good look at me at all.

My dad's car pulled up the drive as I reached the front porch. I went tearing after him, running around the side of the house to the back.

"Dad! Hi!" I called as he climbed out of the car.

"Hey, how's it going?" he asked. His suit was rumpled. His hair was disheveled. He looked tired.

"Dad, can we get this film developed — right away?" I demanded, shoving the camera toward him.

"Whoa!" he cried. "I just got home. Let's talk about it at dinner, okay?"

"No, Dad — really!" I insisted. "I have to get this developed. There's something very important on it."

He walked past me toward the house, his shoes crunching over the gravel driveway.

I followed right behind, still holding my camera up high. "Please, Dad? It's really important. Really really important!"

He turned, chuckling. "What have you got? A picture of that boy who moved across the street?"

"No," I replied angrily. "I'm serious, Dad. Can't you take me to the mall? There's that one-hour developing place there."

"What's so important?" he asked, his smile fading. He ran a hand over his head, smoothing down his thick, black hair.

I had the urge to tell him. I had the urge to tell him I had a photo of the monster in there. But I stopped myself.

I knew he wouldn't believe me. I knew he wouldn't take me seriously.

And then he wouldn't drive me to the mall to get my film developed. No way.

"I'll show it to you when it's developed," I said.

He held open the screen door. We walked into the kitchen. Dad sniffed the air a couple of times, expecting the aroma of cooking food.

Mom came bursting in from the hallway to greet us. "Don't sniff," she told my dad. "There's nothing cooking. We're eating out tonight."

"Great!" I cried. "Can we eat at the mall? At that Chinese restaurant you like?" I turned to my Dad. "Please? Please? Then I could get my film developed while we eat."

"I could go for Chinese food," Mom said thoughtfully. Then she turned her gaze on me. "Why so eager to get your film developed?"

"It's a secret," Dad said before I could reply. "She won't tell."

I couldn't hold it in any longer. "It's a picture I snapped of Mr. Mortman," I told them excitedly. "It's my proof that he's a monster."

Mom rolled her eyes. Dad shook his head.

"It's proof!" I insisted. "Maybe when you see the photo, you'll finally believe me."

"You're right," Dad said sarcastically. "I'll believe it when I see it."

"Randy! Hurry downstairs!" Mom shouted into the hallway. "We're going to the mall for Chinese food!"

"Aw, do we *have* to have Chinese food?" my brother called down unhappily. His standard reply.

"I'll get you the plain *lo mein* noodles you like," Mom called up to him. "Just hurry. We're all hungry."

I pushed the button on my camera to rewind the roll of film. "I'm going to drop this at the one-hour developing place before dinner," I told them. "Then we can pick it up after dinner."

"No monster talk at dinner tonight — promise?" Mom said sternly. "I don't want you scaring your brother."

"Promise," I said, pulling the film roll out of the camera, squeezing it between my fingers.

After dinner, I told myself, *I won't have to talk about monsters — I'll show you one!*

Dinner seemed to take forever.

Randy didn't stop complaining the whole time. He said his noodles tasted funny. He said the spareribs were too greasy, and the soup was too hot. He spilled his glass of water all over the table.

I barely paid any attention to what anyone said. I was thinking about my snapshot. I couldn't wait to see it — and to show it to Mom and Dad.

I could just imagine the looks on their faces when they saw that I was right, that I hadn't been making it up — that Mr. Mortman really was a monster.

I imagined both my parents apologizing to me, promising they'd never doubt me again.

"I feel so bad," I imagined my dad saying, "I'm going to buy you that computer you've been asking for."

"And a new bike," I imagined Mom saying. "Please forgive us for doubting you."

"And I'm sorry, too," I imagined Randy saying. "I know I've been a real jerk."

"And you can stay up till midnight every night from now on, even on school nights," I imagined Dad saying.

Suddenly, my mom's voice broke into my daydreams. "Lucy, I don't think you heard a word I said," she scolded.

"No . . . I . . . uh . . . was thinking about something," I admitted. I picked up my chopsticks and raised a chunk of rice to my mouth.

"She was thinking about *monsters!*" Randy cried, raising both hands up over the table, squeezing his fingers as if he were a monster about to attack me.

"No monster talk!" Mom insisted sharply.

"Don't look at me!" I cried. "He said it — not me!" I pointed an accusing finger at Randy.

"Just finish your dinner," Dad said quietly. He had sparerib grease all over his chin.

Finally, we were opening our fortune cookies. Mine said something about waiting for sunshine when the clouds part. I never *get* those fortunes.

Dad paid the check. Randy nearly spilled another glass of water as we were standing up. I went running out of the restaurant. I was so excited, so eager, I couldn't wait another second.

The little photo store was on the upper level. I leapt onto the escalator, grabbed the rail, and rode to the top. Then I tore into the store, up to the counter, and called breathlessly to the young woman at the developing machine, "Are my photos ready yet?"

She turned, startled by my loud voice. "I think so. What's your name?"

I told her. She walked over to a rack of yellow envelopes and began slowly shuffling through them.

I tapped my fingers nervously on the countertop, staring at the stack of yellow envelopes. *Couldn't she hurry it up a little?*

She shuffled all the way through the stack, then turned back to me. "What did you say your name was again?"

Trying not to sound too exasperated, I told her my name again. I leaned eagerly on the countertop, my heart pounding, and stared at her as she began once again to shuffle through the yellow envelopes, moving her lips as she read the names.

Finally, she pulled one out and handed it to me.

I grabbed it and started to tear it open.

"That comes to fourteen dollars even," she said.

I realized I didn't have any money. "I'll have to

get my dad," I told her, not letting go of the precious package.

I turned, and Dad appeared in the doorway. Mom and Randy waited outside.

He paid.

I carried the envelope of photos out of the store. My hands were shaking as I pulled it open and removed the snapshots.

"Lucy, calm down," Mom said, sounding worried.

I stared down at the snapshots. All photos of Randy's birthday party.

I sifted through them quickly, staring at the grinning faces of Randy's stupid friends.

Where is it? Where is it? Where is it?

Of course, it was the very last photo, the one on the bottom of the stack.

"Here it is!" I cried.

Mom and Dad leaned forward to see over my shoulder.

The other photos fell from my hand and scattered over the floor as I raised the photo to my face —

— and gasped.

17

The photo was clear and sharp.

Mr. Mortman's large desk stood in the center in a burst of bright light. I could see papers on the desk, the pan of turtles at the far corner, a low pile of books.

Behind the desk, I could see the top of Mr. Mortman's tall wooden stool. And behind the stool, the shelves were in clear focus, even the glass jar of flies on the lower shelf.

But there was no monster.

No Mr. Mortman.

No one.

No one in the snapshot at all.

"He — he was standing right there!" I cried. "Beside the desk!"

"The room looks empty," Dad said, staring down over my shoulder at the snapshot in my quivering hand.

"There's no one there," Mom said, turning her gaze on me.

"He was there," I insisted, unable to take my eyes off the photo. "Right there." I pointed to where the monster had stood.

Randy laughed. "Let me see." He pulled the photo from my hand and examined it. "I see him!" he declared. "He's invisible!"

"It isn't funny," I said weakly. I pulled the photo away from him. I sighed unhappily. I felt so bad. I wanted to sink into a hole in the floor and never come out.

"He's invisible!" Randy repeated gleefully, enjoying his own joke.

Mom and Dad were staring at me, looks of concern on their faces.

"Don't you see?" I cried, waving the photo in one hand. "Don't you see? This *proves* it! This proves he's a monster. He doesn't show up in photographs!"

Dad shook his head and frowned. "Lucy, haven't you carried this joke far enough?"

Mom put a hand on my shoulder. "I'm starting to get worried about you," she said softly. "I think you're really starting to believe in your own monster joke."

"Can we get ice cream?" Randy asked.

* * *

101

"I can't believe we're doing this," Aaron complained.

"Just shut up. You *owe* me!" I snapped.

It was the next evening. We were crouched low, hiding behind the low shrubs at the side of the library.

It was a crisp, cool day. The sun was already lowering itself behind the trees. The shadows stretched long and blue over the library lawn.

"I owe you?" Aaron protested. "Are you crazy?"

"You owe me," I repeated. "You were supposed to come to the library with me yesterday, remember. You let me down."

He brushed a bug off his freckled nose. "Can I help it if I had an orthodontist appointment?" He sounded funny. His words were coming out all sticky. He wasn't used to his new braces yet.

"Yes," I insisted. "I counted on you, and you let me down — and you got me in all kinds of trouble."

"What kind of trouble?" He dropped to the ground and sat cross-legged, keeping his head low behind the evergreen shrub.

"My parents said I'm never again allowed to mention Mr. Mortman or the fact that he's a monster," I told him.

"Good," Aaron said.

"Not good. It means I really need you, Aaron. I need you to see that I'm telling the truth, and tell my parents." My voice broke. "They think I'm crazy. They really do!"

He started to reply, but he could see I was really upset. So he stopped himself.

A cool breeze swept past, making the trees all seem to whisper at us.

I kept my eyes trained on the library door. It was five-twenty. Past closing time. Mr. Mortman should be coming out any second.

"So we're going to follow Mr. Mortman home?" Aaron asked, scratching the back of his neck. "And spy on him at his house? Why don't we just watch him through the library window?"

"The window is too high," I replied. "We have to follow him. He told me he walks home every evening. I want you to see him turn into a monster," I said, staring straight ahead over the top of the bush. "I want you to believe me."

"What if I just *say* I believe you?" Aaron asked, grinning. "Then could we just go home?"

"Ssshhh!" I pressed a hand over Aaron's mouth.

The library door was opening. Mr. Mortman appeared on the front steps.

Aaron and I ducked down lower.

I peered through the branches of the shrub. The librarian turned to lock the front door. He was wearing a red-and-white-striped short-sleeved sportshirt and baggy gray slacks. He had a red baseball cap on his bald head.

"Stay far behind," I whispered to Aaron. "Don't let him see you."

"Good advice," Aaron said sarcastically.

We both shifted onto our knees and waited for Mr. Mortman to head down the sidewalk. He hesitated on the steps, replacing the keys in his pants pocket. Then, humming to himself, he walked down the driveway and turned away from us.

"What's he humming about?" Aaron whispered.

"He always hums," I whispered back. Mr. Mortman was more than half a block away. "Let's go," I said, climbing quickly to my feet.

Keeping in the shadows of the trees and shrubs, I began following the librarian. Aaron followed just behind me.

"Do you know where he lives?" Aaron asked.

I turned back to him, frowning. "If I knew where he lived, we wouldn't have to follow him — would we!"

"Oh. Right."

Following someone was a lot harder than I thought. We had to cut through front yards. Some of them had barking dogs. Some had lawn sprinklers going. Some had thick hedges we somehow had to duck through.

At every street corner, Mr. Mortman would stop and look both ways for oncoming cars. Each time, I was certain he was going to look over his shoulder, too, and see Aaron and me creeping along behind him.

He lived farther from the library than I had thought. After several blocks, the houses ended, and a bare, flat field spread in front of us.

Mr. Mortman cut through the field, walking quickly, swinging his stubby arms rhythmically with each step. We had no choice but to follow him across the field. There were no hiding places. No shrubs to duck behind. No hedges to shield us.

We were completely out in the open. We just had to pray that he didn't turn around in the middle of the field and see us.

A block of small, older houses stood beyond the field. Most of the houses were brick, set close to the street on tiny front yards.

Mr. Mortman turned onto a block of these houses. Aaron and I crouched behind a mailbox and watched him walk up to a house near the middle of the block. He stepped onto the small front stoop and fiddled in his pocket for the keys.

"We're here," I whispered to Aaron. "We made it."

"My friend Ralph lives on this block, I think," Aaron said.

"Who cares?" I snapped. "Keep your mind on business, okay?"

We waited until Mr. Mortman had disappeared through the front door of his house, then crept closer.

His house was white clapboard, badly in need of a paint job. He had a small rectangle of a front yard, with recently cut grass bordered by a single row of tall, yellow tiger lilies.

Aaron and I made our way quickly to the side of the house where there was a narrow strip of grass that led to the back. The window near the front of the house was high enough for us to stand under and not be seen.

A light came on in the window. "That must be his living room," I whispered.

Aaron had a frightened expression. His freckles seemed a lot paler than usual. "I don't like this," he said.

"The hard part was following him," I assured Aaron. "This part is easy. We just watch him through the window."

"But the window is too high," Aaron pointed out. "We can't see anything."

He was right. Staring up from beneath the window, all I could see was the living room ceiling.

"We'll have to stand on something," I said.

"Huh? What?"

I could see Aaron was going to be no help. He was so frightened, his nose was twitching like a bunny rabbit's. I decided if I could keep him busy,

106

maybe I could keep him from totally freaking and running away.

"Go in back. See if there's a ladder or something," I whispered, motioning toward the back of the house.

Another light came on, this one in a back window. Probably the kitchen, I figured. It was also too high to see into.

"Wait. What about that?" Aaron asked. I followed his gaze to a wheelbarrow, tilted against the side of the house.

"Yeah. Maybe," I said. "Bring it over. I'll try to stand on it."

Keeping his head and shoulders bent low, Aaron scampered over to the wheelbarrow. He lifted it away from the house by the handles, then pushed it under the front window.

"Hold it steady," I said.

He grabbed the wooden handles, gazing up at me fearfully. "You sure about this?"

"I'll give it a try," I said, glancing up at the high window.

Holding onto Aaron's shoulder, I gave myself a boost onto the wheelbarrow. He held firmly to the handles as I struggled to find my balance inside the metal basket part.

"It — it's kind of tilty," I whispered, pressing one hand against the side of the house to steady myself.

"I'm doing the best I can," Aaron grumbled.

"There. I think I can stand," I said. I wasn't very high off the ground, but I wasn't at all comfortable. A wheelbarrow is a difficult thing to stand on.

Somewhere down the block a dog barked. I hoped he wasn't barking because of Aaron and me.

Another dog, closer to us, quickly joined in, and it became a barking conversation.

"Are you high enough? Can you see anything?" Aaron asked.

One hand still pressed against the side of the house, I raised my head and peered into the house through the bottom of the window.

"Yeah. I can see some," I called down. "There's a big aquarium in front of the window, but I can see most of the living room."

And just as I said that, Mr. Mortman's face loomed inches from mine.

He was staring right at me!

18

I gasped and lost my balance.

I toppled to the ground, knocking over the wheelbarrow, landing hard on my knees and elbows. "Ow!"

"What happened?" Aaron cried, alarmed.

"He saw me!" I choked out, waiting for the pain to stop throbbing.

"Huh?" Aaron's mouth dropped open.

We both gazed up at the window. I expected to see Mr. Mortman staring down at us.

But no. No sign of him.

I climbed quickly to my feet. "Maybe he was looking at his aquarium," I whispered, motioning for Aaron to set up the wheelbarrow. "Maybe he didn't see me."

"Wh-what are you going to do?" Aaron stammered.

"Get back up, of course," I told him. My legs were shaking as I climbed back onto the wheelbarrow. I grabbed the window ledge and pulled myself up.

The sun had nearly gone down. The darkness outside made it easier to see inside the house. And, I hoped, harder for Mr. Mortman to see out.

I didn't have the best view in the world, I quickly realized. The aquarium, crowded with colorful tropical fish, blocked my view of most of the room.

If only I were a little higher, I thought, I could see over it. But if I *had* been higher, I realized, Mr. Mortman would have seen me.

"What's he doing?" Aaron asked in a trembling whisper.

"Nothing. He's . . . wait!"

Mr. Mortman was staring down at the fish. He stood only a few feet from me, on the other side of the aquarium.

I froze, pressing my hands against the side of the house.

He gazed down into his aquarium, and a smile formed on his pudgy face. He had removed the red baseball cap. His bald head looked yellow in the living room lamplight.

His mouth moved. He was saying something to the tropical fish in the aquarium. I couldn't hear him through the glass.

Then, as he smiled down at his fish, he began to change.

"He's doing it," I whispered to Aaron. "He's turning into a monster."

As I watched Mr. Mortman's head inflate and his eyes bulge out, I was filled with all kinds of strange feelings. I was terrified. And I was fascinated. It was exciting to be so close, inches away from a real monster.

And I felt so happy and relieved that Aaron would finally see for himself that I was telling the truth.

Then, as Mr. Mortman's mouth grew wider and began to gyrate, a twisting black hole on his swollen, yellow face, fear overtook me. I froze there, my face pressed against the window, not blinking, not moving.

I stared as he reached a hand into the aquarium.

His fat fingers wrapped around a slender blue fish. He pulled it up and flipped it into his mouth. I could see long, yellow teeth inside the enormous mouth, biting down, chewing the wriggling fish.

Then, as I gaped in growing terror, Mr. Mortman pulled a black snail off the side of the aquarium glass. Holding its shell between his fingertips, he stuffed the snail into his mouth. His teeth crunched down hard on the shell, cracking it — a crack so loud, I could hear it through the window glass.

My stomach churned. I felt sick.

He swallowed the snail, then reached to pull

another one off the aquarium glass.

"I think I'm going to toss my lunch," I whispered down to Aaron.

Aaron.

I had forgotten all about him.

I was so fascinated by the monster, so excited, so terrified to watch him close up, I had forgotten the whole purpose of being here.

"Aaron, help me down," I whispered. "Quick."

Still staring through the window, I reached a hand down for Aaron to take it.

"Aaron — hurry! Help me down so you can climb up here. You have to see this! You have to see the monster!"

He didn't reply.

"Aaron? Aaron?"

I lowered my eyes from the window.

Aaron had disappeared.

19

I felt a stab of panic in my chest.

My entire body convulsed in a tremor of cold fear.

Where was he?

Had he run away?

Was Aaron so frightened that he just took off without telling me?

Or had something happened to him? Something really bad?

"Aaron? Aaron?" In my panic, I forgot that I was inches away from a monster, and started to shout. "Aaron? Where *are* you?"

"Ssh," I heard a whisper from the back of the house. Aaron appeared, making his way quickly toward me along the narrow strip of grass. "I'm right here, Lucy."

"Huh? Where'd you go?"

He pointed to the back. "I thought maybe I

could find a ladder or something. You know. So I could see, too."

"You scared me to death!" I cried.

I returned my glance to the window. Mr. Mortman was sucking a slithering eel into his mouth like a strand of spaghetti.

"Quick, Aaron — help me down," I instructed, still feeling shaken from the scare of his disappearance. "You have to see this. You have to. Before he changes back."

"He — he's really a monster?" Aaron's mouth dropped open. "You're not joking?"

"Just get up here!" I cried impatiently.

But as I tried to lower myself to the ground, the wheelbarrow slid out from under me.

It toppled onto its side, the handles scraping the side of the house.

My hands shot up to grab the windowsill. I missed and fell heavily on top of the wheelbarrow. "Ow!" I cried out as sharp pain cut through my side.

Glancing up, I saw the monster's startled face, goggling down at me through the glass.

I scrambled to get up. But the throbbing pain in my side took my breath away.

"Aaron — help me!"

But he was already running to the street, his sneakers scraping the grass, his arms stretched straight in front of him as if trying to grab onto safety.

Ignoring the pain in my side, I scrambled to my feet.

I took an unsteady step, then another. I shook my head, trying to shake away my dizziness.

Then I sucked in a deep breath and started to run, following Aaron toward the street.

I had gone about four or five steps when I felt Mr. Mortman's surprisingly strong hands grab my shoulders from behind.

20

I tried to scream, but no sound came out.

He held firmly onto my shoulders. I could feel his hot, wet hands through my T-shirt.

I tried to pull away, but he was too strong.

He spun me around.

His face was back to normal.

He squinted at me with those little black eyes, as if he couldn't believe what he was seeing. "Lucy!" he exclaimed in his scratchy voice.

He let go of my shoulders and stepped back.

I was panting loudly. I was so frightened, my chest felt about to explode.

How had he changed back from his monster form so quickly?

What was he going to do to me?

"Lucy, good heavens. I thought you were a burglar," he said, shaking his head. He removed a white handkerchief from his back pocket and wiped his perspiring forehead.

"S-sorry," I stammered. My voice came out in a choked whisper.

He balled up the handkerchief between his fat hands and jammed it back into his pocket. "What are you doing here?"

"Well . . ." My heart was pounding so hard, I could feel the blood pulse at my temples. My side still ached from where I had fallen on the wheelbarrow.

I struggled to clear my mind. I had to think of an answer to his question. I *had* to.

"Well . . ." I started again, thinking desperately. "I . . . uh . . . came to tell you that I'll . . . uh . . . be a little late for my Reading Rangers appointment tomorrow."

He narrowed his eyes and stared at me thoughtfully. "But why were you looking through my window?" he demanded.

"Well . . . I just . . ."

Think, Lucy — think!

"I didn't know if you were home or not. I just was trying to see if you were there. I mean. So I could tell you. About the appointment tomorrow."

Staring into his face, trying to sound sincere, I took a step back, in case I had to make a run for it.

Did he believe me?

Was he buying it?

I couldn't tell. He continued to stare at me thoughtfully.

He rubbed his chins. "You really didn't have to come all the way out here," he said softly. "Did you ride your bike?" His eyes darted over the small front lawn.

"No. I . . . uh . . . walked. I like to walk," I replied awkwardly.

"It's getting dark," he said. "Maybe you should call your mom or dad to come pick you up. Why don't you come inside and use the phone?"

Come inside?

Come inside the monster's house?

No way!

"Uh . . . no thanks, Mr. Mortman," I said, taking another step backwards toward the street. "My parents don't mind if I walk home. It isn't that far. Really."

"No. I insist," he said, an odd grin starting across his molelike face. He motioned toward the house. "Come on in, Lucy. The phone is in the living room," he urged. "Come on. I won't bite."

I shuddered.

I'd just seen him bite snails. And eels.

There was no way I was going in that house. I knew that if I went in, chances are I'd never come out.

"I — I've got to go," I said, giving him a wave of one hand. I could feel the fear creeping up my back, running over my body. I knew if I didn't get away from there — *that moment* — I'd be frozen by my terror, unable to escape.

"Lucy — " Mr. Mortman insisted.

"No. Really. Bye, Mr. Mortman." I waved again, turned, and started jogging to the street.

"You really shouldn't have come all this way!" he called after me in his high, scratchy voice. "Really. You shouldn't have!"

I know! I thought. *I know I shouldn't have.*

I trotted along the street, turned the corner, and continued down the next block.

Was I really getting away?

Was he really letting me go?

I couldn't believe he'd bought my lame excuse. Why was he letting me get away?

I slowed to a walk. My side still ached. I suddenly had a throbbing headache.

Night had fallen. Passing cars had their headlights on. A slender trail of dark cloud drifted over a pale half-moon still low in the purple-gray sky.

I was about to cross the street onto the broad, empty field when hands grabbed my shoulders again.

I cried out, more of a *yelp* than a scream, and spun around, expecting to see the monster.

"Aaron!" I cried. I swallowed hard, trying to force down my fear. "Where — ?"

"I waited for you," he said. His voice trembled.

119

His hands were knotted into fists. He looked about ready to burst into tears.

"Aaron — "

"I've been waiting all this time," he said shrilly. "Where've you been? I've been so scared."

"I was . . . back there," I told him.

"I was ready to call the police or something," Aaron said. "I was hiding down the block. I — "

"You saw him?" I asked eagerly, suddenly remembering why we had risked our lives tonight. "You saw Mr. Mortman?"

Aaron shook his head. "No, I didn't. I was too far away."

"But earlier," I said. "Through the window. When he was a monster. Didn't you see him then? Didn't you see him eat the snails and the eels?"

Aaron shook his head again. "I didn't see anything, Lucy," he said softly. "I'm sorry. I wish I had."

Big help, I thought bitterly.

Now what was I going to do?

21

"Mom — you don't understand. I *can't* go!"

"Lucy, I'm not giving you a choice. You're going, and that's that."

It was the next afternoon, a stormy, gray day, and Mom and I were in the kitchen, arguing. I was trying to tell her there was no way I could go to my Reading Rangers meeting at the library. And she was insisting that I had to go.

"Mom, you've got to believe me," I pleaded. I was trying not to whine, but my voice kept creeping higher and higher. "Mr. Mortman is a monster. I can't go to the library anymore."

Mom made a disgusted face and tossed down the dish towel she'd been folding. "Lucy, your father and I have had it up to here with your silly monster stories."

She turned to face me. Her expression was angry. "The fact is, Lucy dear, that you are a quitter. You never stick with anything. You're lazy. That's your problem."

"Mr. Mortman is a monster," I interrupted. *"That's* my problem."

"Well, I don't care," Mom replied sharply. "I don't care if he turns into a drooling werewolf at night. You're not quitting Reading Rangers. You're going to your appointment this afternoon if I have to take you by the hand and walk you there myself."

"Gee — would you?" I asked.

The idea flashed into my head that Mom could hide in the stacks and see for herself when Mr. Mortman turned into a monster.

But I guess she thought I was being sarcastic. She just scowled and walked out of the kitchen.

And so, an hour later, I was trudging up the stone steps to the old library. It was raining hard, but I didn't take an umbrella. I didn't care if I got drenched.

My hair was soaked and matted on my head. I shook my head hard as I stepped into the entryway, sending drops of water flying in all directions.

I shivered, more from my fear, from being back in this frightening place, than from the cold. I pulled off my backpack. It was dripping wet, too.

How can I face Mr. Mortman? I wondered as I made my way reluctantly into the main reading room. How can I face him after last night?

He must surely suspect that I know his secret.

He *couldn't* have believed me last night, could he?

I was so furious at my mom for forcing me to come here.

I hope he turns into a monster and chews me to bits! I thought bitterly. That will really teach Mom a lesson.

I pictured Mom and Dad and Randy, sitting mournfully in our living room, crying their eyes out, wailing, "If only we had believed her! If only we had listened!"

Holding my wet backpack in front of me like a shield, I made my way slowly past the long rows of books to the front of the room.

To my relief, there were several people in the library. I saw two little kids with their mothers and a couple of other women browsing in the mystery book section.

Great! I thought, starting to feel a little calmer. Mr. Mortman won't dare do anything while the library is filled with people.

The librarian was dressed in a green turtleneck today, which really made him look like a big, round turtle. He was stamping a stack of books and didn't look up as I stepped close to the desk.

I cleared my throat nervously. "Mr. Mortman?"

It took him a long while to look up. When he

finally did, a warm smile formed above his chins. "Hi, Lucy. Give me a few minutes, okay?"

"Sure," I said. "I'll go dry off."

He seems very friendly, I thought, heading over to a chair at one of the long tables. He doesn't seem angry at all.

Maybe he really did believe my story last night.

Maybe he really doesn't know that I've seen him turn into a monster.

Maybe I'll get out of here alive. . . .

I sat down at the table and shook some more water from my hair. I stared at the big, round wall clock, nervously waiting for him to call me up for our meeting. The clock ticked noisily. Each second seemed to take a minute.

The kids with their mothers checked out some books and left. I turned to the mystery section and saw that the two women had also cleared out. The librarian and I were the only ones left.

Mr. Mortman shoved a stack of books across his desk and stood up. "I'll be right back, Lucy," he said, another friendly, reassuring smile on his face. "Then we'll have our meeting."

He stepped away from his desk and, walking briskly, headed to the back of the reading room. I guessed he was going to the bathroom or something.

A jagged flash of white lightning flickered

across the dark sky outside the window. It was followed by a drumroll of thunder.

I stood up from the table and, carrying my wet backpack by the straps, started toward Mr. Mortman's desk.

I was halfway to the desk when I heard the loud click.

I knew at once that he had locked the front door.

A few seconds later, he returned, walking briskly, still smiling. He was rubbing his pudgy white hands together as he walked.

"Shall we talk about your book?" he asked, stepping up to me.

"Mr. Mortman — you locked the front door," I said, swallowing hard.

His smile didn't fade.

His dark little eyes locked on mine.

"Yes. Of course," he said softly, studying my face. His hands were still clasped together in front of him.

"But — why?" I stammered.

He brought his face close to mine, and his smile faded. "I know why you were at my house last night," he growled into my ear. "I know everything."

"But, Mr. Mortman, 1 — "

"I'm sorry," he said in his throaty growl. "But I can't let you leave, Lucy. I can't let you leave the library."

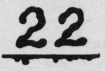

22

"Ohhh." The sound escaped my lips, a moan of total terror.

I stared at him without moving. I guess I wanted to see if he was serious or not. If he really meant what he said.

His eyes told me he did.

And as I stared at him, his head began to inflate. His tiny, round eyes shot out of their sockets and grew into throbbing, black bulbs.

"Ohhh."

Again, the terrified sound escaped my lips. My entire body convulsed in a shudder of terror.

His head was throbbing now, throbbing like a heart. His mouth opened into a gaping, gruesome leer, and green spittle ran down his quivering chin.

Move! I told myself. *Move, Lucy! DO something!*

His disgusting grin grew wider. His enormous

head bobbed and throbbed excitedly.

He uttered a low growl of attack. And reached out both arms to grab me.

"No!" I shrieked.

I leaned back and, with all my might, swung the backpack into his flabby stomach.

It caught him by surprise.

He gasped as it took his breath away.

I let go of the backpack, spun around, and started to run.

He was right behind me. I could hear his panting breath and low, menacing growls.

I ran through a narrow aisle between two tall shelves.

A rumble of thunder from outside seemed to shake the room.

He was still behind me. Close. Closer.

He was going to catch me, going to grab me from behind.

I reached the end of the row. I hesitated. I didn't know which way to turn. I couldn't think.

He roared, a monstrous animal sound.

I turned left and started to run along the back wall of the room.

Another rumble of thunder.

"Ohh!" I realized to my horror that I'd made a mistake.

A fatal mistake.

I was running right into the corner.

There was no exit here. No escape.

He roared again, so loud that it drowned out the thunder.

I was trapped.

I knew it.

Trapped.

With a desperate cry, I ran blindly — headlong into the card catalogue.

Behind me, I heard the monster's roar of laughter.

He knew he had won.

23

The card catalogue toppled over. Drawers came sliding out. Cards spilled at my feet, scattering over the floor.

"Noooo!" the monster howled. At first I thought it was a victory cry. But then I realized it was an angry cry of protest.

With a moan of horror, he stooped to the floor and began gathering up the cards.

Staring in disbelief, I plunged past him, running frantically, my arms thrashing wildly at my sides.

In that moment of terror, I remembered the one thing that librarians hate most: having cards from the card catalogue spilled on the floor!

Mr. Mortman was a monster — but he was also a librarian.

He couldn't bear to have those cards in disorder. He had to try to replace them before chasing after me.

It took only seconds to run into the front entryway, turn the lock, pull open the door, and flee out into the rain.

My sneakers slapped the pavement as I ran, sending up splashes of rainwater.

I made my way to the street and was halfway up the block when I realized he was chasing after me.

A flash of lightning crackled to my left.

I cried out, startled, as a deafening burst of thunder shook the ground.

I glanced back to see how close the monster was.

And stopped.

With trembling hands, I frantically brushed a glaze of rainwater from my eyes.

"Aaron!" I cried. "What are *you* doing here?"

He ran up to me, hunching against the cold rain. He was breathing hard. His eyes were wide and frightened. "I — I was in the library," he stammered, struggling to catch his breath. "Hiding. I saw it. I saw the monster. I saw everything."

"You *did?*" I was so happy. I wanted to hug him.

A sheet of rain swept over us, driven by a gust of wind.

"Let's get to my house!" I cried. "You can tell my parents. Now maybe they'll finally believe it!"

* * *

Aaron and I burst into the den. Mom looked up from the couch, lowering the newspaper to her lap. "You're dripping on the rug," she said.

"Where's Dad? Is he home yet?" I asked, rainwater running down my forehead. Aaron and I were soaked from head to foot.

"Here I am." He appeared behind us. He had changed out of his work clothes. "What's all the excitement?"

"It's about the monster!" I blurted out. "Mr. Mortman — he — "

Mom shook her head and started to raise a hand to stop me.

But Aaron quickly came to my rescue. "I saw him, too!" Aaron exclaimed. "Lucy didn't make it up. It's true!"

Mom and Dad listened to Aaron. I knew they would.

He told them what he had seen in the library. He told them how the librarian had turned into a monster and chased me into the corner.

Mom listened intently to Aaron's story, shaking her head. "I guess Lucy's story is true," she said when Aaron had finished.

"Yeah. I guess it is," Dad said, putting a hand gently on my shoulder.

"Well, now that you *finally* believe me — what are you going to do, Dad?" I demanded.

He gazed at me thoughtfully. "We'll invite Mr. Mortman for dinner," he said.

"Huh?" I goggled at him, rainwater running down my face. "You'll *what*? He tried to gobble me up! You *can't* invite him here!" I protested. "You can't!"

"Lucy, we have no choice," Dad insisted. "We'll invite him for dinner."

24

Mr. Mortman arrived a few evenings later, carrying a bouquet of flowers. He was wearing lime-green trousers and a bright yellow, short-sleeved sport shirt.

Mom accepted the flowers from him and led him into the living room where Dad, Randy, and I were waiting. I gripped the back of a chair tightly as he entered. My legs felt rubbery, and my stomach felt as if I'd swallowed a heavy rock.

I *still* couldn't believe that Dad had invited Mr. Mortman into our house!

Dad stepped forward to shake hands with the librarian. "We've been meaning to invite you for quite a while," Dad told him, smiling. "We want to thank you for the excellent reading program at the library."

"Yes," Mom joined in. "It's really meant a lot to Lucy."

Mr. Mortman glanced at me uncertainly. I could

see that he was studying my expression. "I'm glad," he said, forcing a tight-lipped smile.

Mr. Mortman lowered himself onto the couch. Mom offered him a tray of crackers with cheese on them. He took one and chewed on it delicately.

Randy sat down on the rug. I was still standing behind the armchair, gripping the back of it so tightly, my hands ached. I had never been so nervous in all my life.

Mr. Mortman seemed nervous, too. When Dad handed him a glass of iced tea, Mr. Mortman spilled a little on his trousers. "It's such a humid day," he said. "This iced tea hits the spot."

"Being a librarian must be interesting work," Mom said, taking a seat beside Mr. Mortman on the couch.

Dad was standing at the side of the couch.

They chatted for a while. As they talked, Mr. Mortman kept darting glances at me. Randy, sitting cross-legged on the floor, drummed his fingers on the carpet.

Mom and Dad seemed calm and perfectly at ease. Mr. Mortman seemed a little uncomfortable. He had glistening beads of perspiration on his shiny, round forehead.

My stomach growled loudly, more from nervousness than from hunger. No one seemed to hear it.

The three adults chatted a while longer. Mr. Mortman sipped his iced tea.

He leaned back on the couch and smiled at my mother. "It was so kind of you to invite me. I don't get too many home-cooked meals. What's for dinner?" he asked.

"*You* are!" my Dad told him, stepping in front of the couch.

"What?" Mr. Mortman raised a hand behind his ear. "I didn't hear you correctly. What is for dinner?"

"*You* are!" Dad repeated.

"Ulllp!" Mr. Mortman let out a little cry and turned bright red. He struggled to raise himself from the low couch.

But Mom and Dad were too fast for him.

They both pounced on him. Their fangs popped down. And they gobbled the librarian up in less than a minute, bones and all.

Randy laughed gleefully.

I had a big smile on my face.

My brother and I haven't gotten our fangs yet. That's why we couldn't join in.

"Well, that's that," Mom said, standing up and straightening the couch cushion. Then she turned to Randy and me. "That's the first monster to come to Timberland Falls in nearly twenty years," she told us. "That's why it took us so long to believe you, Lucy."

"You sure gobbled him up fast!" I exclaimed.

"In a few years, you'll get your fangs," Mom said.

"Me, too!" Randy declared. "Then maybe I won't be afraid of monsters anymore!"

Mom and Dad chuckled. Then Mom's expression turned serious. "You both understand why we had to do that, don't you? We can't allow any *other* monsters in town. It would frighten the whole community. And we don't *want* people to get frightened and chase us away. We like it here!"

Dad burped loudly. "Pardon me," he said, covering his mouth.

Later that night, I was upstairs in Randy's room. He was all tucked in, and I was telling him a bedtime story.

". . . And so the librarian hid behind the tall bookshelf," I said in a low, whispery voice. "And when the little boy named Randy reached up to pull a book down from the shelf, the librarian stuck his long arms through the shelf and *grabbed* the boy, and — "

"Lucy, how many times do I have to tell you?"

I glanced up to see Mom standing in the doorway, a frown on her face.

"I don't want you frightening your little brother before bedtime," Mom scolded. "You'll give him nightmares. Now, come on, Lucy — no more monster stories!"

Add *more*

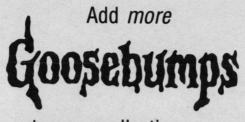

to your collection . . .
A chilling preview of
what's next from
R.L. STINE

WELCOME TO CAMP NIGHTMARE

5

Mike was right beneath me, making his bed. He screamed so loud, I cried out and nearly fell off the ladder.

I leapt off the ladder, my heart pounding, and stepped beside him.

Staring straight ahead, his mouth wide open in horror, Mike backed away from his bed.

"Mike — what's wrong?" I asked. "What *is* it?"

"S-snakes!" Mike stammered, staring straight ahead at his unmade bed as he backed away.

"Huh?" I followed his gaze. It was too dark to see anything.

Colin laughed. "Not *that* old joke!" he cried.

"Larry put rubber snakes in your bed," Jay said, grinning as he stepped up beside us.

"They're not rubber! They're real!" Mike insisted, his voice trembling.

Jay laughed and shook his head. "I can't believe you fell for that old gag." He took a few steps toward the bed — then stopped. "Hey — !"

I moved close, and the two snakes came into focus. Raising themselves from the shadows, they arched their slender heads, pulling back as if preparing to attack.

"They're real!" Jay cried, turning back to Colin. "Two of them!"

"Probably not poisonous," Colin said, venturing closer.

The two let out angry hisses, raising themselves high off the bed. They were very long and skinny. Their heads were wider than their bodies. Their tongues flicked from side to side as they arched themselves menacingly.

"I'm scared of snakes," Mike uttered in a soft voice.

"They're probably scared of you!" Jay joked, slapping Mike on the back.

Mike winced. He was in no mood for Jay's horseplay. "We've got to get Larry or somebody," Mike said.

"No way!" Jay insisted. "You can handle 'em, Mike. There's only two of them!"

Jay gave Mike a playful shove toward the bed. He only meant to give him a scare.

But Mike stumbled — and fell onto the bed.

The snakes darted in unison.

I saw one of them clamp its teeth into Mike's hand.

Mike raised himself to his feet. He didn't react at first. Then he uttered a high-pitched shriek.

Two drops of blood appeared on the back of his right hand. He stared down at them, then grabbed the hand.

"It *bit* me!" he shrieked.

"Oh, no!" I cried.

"Did it puncture the skin?" Colin asked. "Is it bleeding?"

Jay rushed forward and grabbed Mike's shoulder. "Hey, man — I'm really sorry," he said. "I didn't mean to — "

Mike groaned in pain. "It — really hurts," he whispered. He was breathing really hard, his chest heaving, making weird noises as he breathed.

The snakes, coiled in the middle of his lower bunk, began to hiss again.

"You'd better hurry to the nurse," Jay said, his hand still on Mike's shoulder. "I'll come with you."

"N-no," Mike stammered. His face was as pale as a ghost. He held his hand tightly. "I'll go find her!" He burst out of the cabin, running at full speed. The door slammed behind him.

"Hey — I didn't mean to push him, you know," Jay explained to us. I could see he was really upset. "I was just joking, just trying to scare him a little. I didn't mean for him to fall or anything. . . ." His voice trailed off.

"What are we going to do about *them*?" I asked, pointing at the two coiled snakes.

"I'll get Larry," Colin offered. He started toward the door.

"No, wait." I called him back. "Look. They're sitting on Mike's sheet, right?"

Jay and Colin followed my gaze to the bed. The snakes arched themselves high, preparing to bite again.

"So?" Jay asked, scratching his disheveled hair.

"So we can wrap them up in the sheet and carry them outside," I said.

Jay stared at me. "Wish I'd thought of that. Let's do it, man!"

"You'll get bit," Colin warned.

I stared at the snakes. They seemed to be studying me, too. "They can't bite us through the sheet," I said.

"They can try!" Colin exclaimed, hanging back.

"If we're fast enough," I said, taking a cautious step toward the bed, "we can wrap them up before they know what's happening."

The snakes hissed out a warning, drawing themselves higher.

"How did they get in here, anyway?" Colin asked.

"Maybe the camp is *crawling* with snakes," Jay said, grinning. "Maybe you've got some in *your* bed, too, Colin!" He laughed.

"Let's get serious here," I said sternly, my eyes locked on the coiled snakes. "Are we going to try this or not?"

"Yeah. Let's do it," Jay answered. "I mean, I owe it to Mike."

Colin remained silent.

"I'll bet I could grab one by the tail and swing him out through the window," Jay said. "You could grab the tail end of the other one and — "

"Let's try my plan first," I suggested quietly.

We crept over to the snakes, sneaking up on them. It was kind of silly since they were staring right at us.

I pointed to one end of the sheet, which was folded up onto the bed. "Grab it there," I instructed Jay. "Then pull it up."

He hesitated. "What if I miss? Or you miss?"

"Then we're in trouble," I replied grimly. My eyes on the snakes, I reached my hand forward to the other corner of the sheet. "Ready? On three," I whispered.

My heart was in my mouth. I could barely choke out, "One, two, three."

At the count of three, we both grabbed for the ends of the sheet.

"Pull!" I cried in a shrill voice I couldn't believe was coming from me.

We pulled up the sheet and brought the ends together, making a bundle.

At the bottom of the bundle, the snakes wriggled frantically. I heard their jaws snap. They wriggled so hard, the bottom of the bundle swung back and forth.

"They don't like this," Jay said as we hurried to the door, carrying our wriggling, swaying bundle between us, trying to keep our bodies as far away from it as possible.

I pushed open the door with my shoulder, and we ran out onto the grass.

"Now what?" Jay asked.

"Keep going," I replied. I could see one of the snakes poking its head out. "Hurry!"

We ran past the cabins toward a small clump of shrubs. Beyond the shrubs stood a patch of low trees. When we reached the trees, we swung the bundle back, then heaved the whole sheet into the trees.

It opened as it fell to the ground. The two snakes slithered out instantly and pulled themselves to shelter under the trees.

Jay and I let out loud sighs of relief. We stood there for a moment, hunched over, hands on our knees, trying to catch our breath.

Crouching down, I looked for the snakes. But they had slithered deep into the safety of the evergreens.

I stood up. "I guess we should take back Mike's sheet," I said.

"He probably won't want to sleep on it," Jay said. But he reached down and pulled it up from the grass. He balled it up and tossed it to me. "It's probably dripping with snake venom," he said, making a disgusted face.

When we got back to the cabin, Colin had made his bed and was busily unpacking the contents of his trunk, shoving everything into the top dresser drawer. He turned as we entered. "How'd it go?" he asked casually.

"Horrible," Jay replied quickly, his expression grim. "We both got bit. Twice."

"You're a terrible liar!" Colin told him, laughing. "You shouldn't even try."

Jay laughed, too.

Colin turned to me. "You're a hero," he said.

"Thanks for all your help," Jay told him sarcastically.

Colin started to reply. But the cabin door opened, and Larry poked his freckled face in. "How's it going?" he asked. "You're not finished yet?"

"We had a little problem," Jay told him.

"Where's the fourth guy? The chubby one?" Larry asked, lowering his head so he wouldn't bump it on the doorframe as he stepped inside.

"Mike got bit. By a snake," I told him.

"There were two snakes in his bed," Jay added.

Larry's expression didn't change. He didn't

seem at all surprised. "So where did Mike go?" he asked casually, swatting a mosquito on his arm.

"His hand was bleeding. He went to the nurse to get it taken care of," I told him.

"Huh?" Larry's mouth dropped open.

"He went to find the nurse," I repeated.

Larry tossed back his head and started to laugh. "Nurse?" he cried, laughing hard. "*What* nurse?!"

About the Author

R.L. STINE is the author of over two dozen best-selling thrillers and mysteries for young people. Recent titles for teenagers include *The Babysitter II*, *Beach House*, *Hit and Run*, and *The Girlfriend*, all published by Scholastic. He is also the author of the *Fear Street* series.

When he isn't writing scary books, he is head writer of the children's TV show *Eureeka's Castle*, seen on Nickelodeon.

Bob lives in New York City with his wife, Jane, and thirteen-year-old son, Matt.

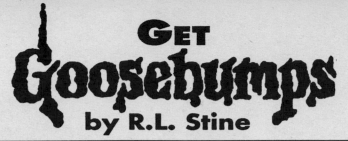